John Brindley was born in London and now lives in Essex. Last year Dolphin published his gripping thriller *The Terrible Quin*. His greatest inspiration has been his children, to whom he tells the stories on camping holidays.

Turning to Stone

JOHN BRINDLEY

Orion Children's Books
and
Dolphin Paperbacks

Thanks to Jakki and to Fiona
for their invaluable criticisms and guidance

First published in Great Britain in 1999
as a Dolphin paperback
by Orion Children's Books
a division of the Orion Publishing Group Ltd
Orion House
5 Upper St Martin's Lane
London WC2H 9EA

A catalogue record for this book
is available from the British Library

Typeset at The Spartan Press Ltd,
Lymington, Hants
Printed in Great Britain by
Clays Ltd, St Ives plc

ISBN 1 85881 638 6

PART ONE

Friday and What Happened Last Night

Friday

Breakfast, mad, or what?

The old man going into one again about the stuff Tom likes to eat every day. It's as if you're supposed to want to feed on muesli and dried fruit and bran and stuff that looks going in more like it should be coming out. None of that sugar-stuff, the old man's always going, no more of that chocolate rubbish.

You know, somewhere along the line, people, parents, they lose all sense of taste. They do. They all do. They soon get to liking eating peas and beetroot and lettuce. They lose the sense of what's good or what's boring on TV – they start watching the news, as if they were looking out for something or the other on it. It makes you wonder what they've done sometimes, they're so worried about what's going on.

And clothes? Just look at the dads in their shell-suits or corduroys of a weekend. Have a look at the way they let that belly hang over the waistband of the jeans. Have you seen them, in the summer, out washing the car? Have you seen the old shorts with an ordinary white shirt open at the neck, black socks and sandals? Have you seen them?

You've got to eat horses' oats and budgie-seed and farm droppings they tell you every day at breakfast. Mad, or what?

Then, just when you reckon you're in for a few minutes watch of the TV behind your big sugary breakfast, guess what?

Dressing-gown, slippers, fag on, tea, toast, it's the woman's turn to start on at you where your old man's just left off.

Parents. What are they like?

Eh?

She wants to know every day why you haven't put on a clean shirt to go to school in. Every day she wants to know why you tie your tie so short, what you've gone and done to your blazer pocket so that it's hanging off. She wants to know always when you're going to do your room.

Do what to it you wonder?

Tom does anyway. He's only just got the room the way he likes it. You know, lived in. Pair of decent football boots over in the corner with a decent few chunks of dried mud round them. Action. Old dried socks. Spray 'em up with aerosol for the armpits, soon kill the smell.

'Have you done your homework?' his mum wants to know.

'He'd better have,' the madman pecks at him from round the side of the paper. He always pipes up at the mention of homework.

'I didn't have none,' Tom tells them.

'I didn't have *any*,' his dad says to him.

'Nor did I,' Tom says.

'No,' his dad goes, 'I mean "I didn't have none," is a double negative. It actually means you had some.'

'I didn't,' goes Tom.

'I know you didn't,' says the old man, 'but that's not what you said.'

Mad, or what?

What can you do? What can you do when your

sister's a lunatic and allowed to get away with it because she's supposed to have got hormones. Hormones, she's supposed to have got. That's why she's allowed to run round the house like crazy, slamming doors and going into one every two minutes. She's always going into one every time she so much as sets eyes on Tom.

Like this morning.

'Stop making that horrible noise,' she's going on at Tom, just because he's down to the chocolate milk left in his bowl. She doesn't get it, does she? She doesn't get it that you've got to get that last little bit of brown milk out of your bowl with the spoon. You've got to slurp it up quicker and quicker as the spoon picks less and less up until there's nothing left in your bowl. It has to be done. It's the rules. You have to do it.

She doesn't get it though, Jazz. How could she? How could she when she's always going round eating nothing all day then pigging out on Turkish Delight then going into one about her spots and eating nothing for days on end.

'Get stuffed,' Tom tells her.

'Get a life,' she tries to tell him.

It doesn't work though. He's got one. A life. If there's one thing Tom's got, he reckons, it's a life. 'You get a life,' he tells Jazz.

'No, you get a life,' she says.

'No,' Tom tells her, 'you get a life without spots and crying and—'

But Tom doesn't get to finish what he's saying because his sister's on him like crazy getting a good dig in before the parents decide to intervene. They intervene, the parents, intervening like mad with the paper going everywhere over the floor and a cup of tea spilt and screaming and crying. And that's only from the old man. Jazz and her mum are like a couple of gone-garrity witches with wild green hair and hormones and finger-nails. The place is an uproar, a mad breakfast cauldron of crazy women and a crushing father busting crockery under his bare knuckles.

Tom's away out of the door with his bag slung over one shoulder and his blazer on the other. He slams the door behind him closing down the sound of wild hormones and affronted testosterone and tea-burnt legs. They're all crazy. They always want him to eat what he doesn't want to, then not to eat what he likes. They want him to wear his shirts for less time than he does, all week usually, and his trousers for longer without making them muddy. They want him to wear his school tie with more length, so that it comes down to his belt, his hair shorter, his finger-nails longer and stop biting them, but his long toe-nails shorter.

They're all mad.

His dad reckons cricket's a better game than football. Cricket! It went on for days. Days! Then, when everyone was bored out of their skulls, it turned out to be a draw. How can you play for days, then get a draw?

Cricket better than football? No way.

Football's the best thing in the world. United. U-ni-ted! U-ni-ted! Come on you Reds! The best team in the world, playing the best game in the world.

U-ni-ted!

Jazz hates football. Jazz hates everything. Except boy-bands. But she especially hates football. Tom doesn't get it. How could anybody hate football? You have to be mad.

Anyway, Jazz is mad, Tom reckons. When he's watching the game on Sky, she wants it turned over so that she can watch one of the Soaps or the other. Mad, or what? So she gives him a hard time. She comes flinging in with finger-nails and hair and all that sharp and bony stuff nobody can fight against. She goes crying to their mum about him if he manages to get one in back. He only ever does it in self-defence.

But Tom's always getting done for something or the other, so it's like this morning – it's like out of the house and down the road slinging on his blazer as he goes, his books and pens falling out of his bag all over the road.

He makes his way to the end of the street where the Bains families live.

Tom Rattigan smiles. He's half hidden in the bushes, waiting for the twins, those two crew-cuts to come by kicking a can along the road, laughing like toad brothers.

But you should see them at school, those two Bainsies. Untouchable? They're bomb-proof.

'Did you do this?' the teachers say. 'Did you set fire to this boy? He says you did.'

'No sir.'

'Did you then?' they go, to the other one. 'He says you did.'

'No he doesn't, sir,' they say. 'He says he did it.'

'I didn't do it,' the other one says. 'I wasn't even there. Ask anyone.'

'Nor me,' adds the other half. 'Ask anyone.'

There are just too many Bainsies to be sure. There's always one too many.

So, are they both to blame? Never. What could anybody do about it? One of them is always innocent. One always guilty. But which?

They're both guilty really. It's just that one of them didn't actually do it. They're always each other's alibi.

You can do what you like, it's always possible to produce witnesses to prove that the guilty party was never there.

But they aren't getting away with this one. No way are they. Tom's going to enjoy this.

He's waiting at the end of the road where they both live. He's going to start on them as soon as he can. Oh yes.

He's always wanted to get one over on those Bainsies. Ever since one of them started shouting out Ratty after him till Tom started to chase him round the school. Every time Tom turned the corner, that runt he was chasing shot away from him. Every time Tom caught up a bit, they'd turn the corner, the Bains was off like a rocket.

Tom chased him for what seemed like about four days round and round the school every playtime until he realised what they were doing. They were changing places, the one not being chased took a short cut through the school, so every time Tom turned the corner, he ended up chasing a different Bains.

Still, you had to hand it to them, it was a pretty good trick. Tom made out he knew all the time. But he still wanted to get them back.

Oh yes.

But as Tom waits down the road for the Bainsies, he notices someone else coming down the way. He shrinks back behind the bushes. He doesn't want his sister Jazz to see him.

Like, he never wants his sister Jazz to see him. As soon as she ever does, it's, well, it's like – listen to this, see what you think. Every morning nearly, when Tom's sitting singing in the loo, she's outside slamming the door nearly down.

'Hurry up,' she's always shouting at him.

Tom's hurrying up isn't he – well, kind of. There's only so much hurrying up you can do. But Jazz has to scream and cry because Tom's singing a song, or because he's blown off a bit loud, which she takes as a very personal insult. Tom's only doing his stuff isn't he, as you do, minding his own business. But Jazz, outside, mad? You've never heard anything like it.

The old man always has to bowl up the stairs to put an end to all the wailing, but he does it by slapping at the bathroom door himself and telling Tom to get a move on.

'Hurry up,' his dad's always yelling.

'He doesn't know how to hurry up,' Jazz is harping.

'I am hurrying up,' he's going.

'He isn't,' Jazz insists. 'He's singing. He's winding me up, Dad,' she whines, wanting to get the old man on her side.

Tom always has to jump off the loo before he wants to, to let her in to do all the weird stuff she does to her face and armpits and that. She's always there, waiting outside for him, or there, on at him when he's watching the footie, or there, when he's dunking his biscuits in orange juice, her disgusted nostrils flared. She's always there disapproving of him, having a go at him, putting him down, shouting him down.

'I hate you,' she sometimes goes to him.

When she does, their mum and dad stop her. When they do, she blames Tom. Her nostrils flare at him. He can't win, really.

So when he spots her prowling down the street as if she's looking for a little brother to stamp on, Tom just shrinks back into the bushes out of her way.

She's clumping down the road with that look on her face, that dead serious, miserable kind of nasty kind of look. She's always got that look nowdays.

The thing is, she didn't used to be like this. She used to be proper – a girl, yeah, but no way a girlie girl. She used to be all right. Tom and Jazz used to have a lot of fun together, making dens and that with their friends, climbing trees, scrumping, having a good time.

But all that was before Jazz started trying to be like all the other girls in her year, listening to boy-bands all day, washing their hair, cluttering up the bathroom, growing boobs, all that. It spoils everything. It's spoiled Jazz. You only have to look at her, the way she's coming down the road right now, the confused, and difficult way she's looking round at something. The way she's looking round at nothing.

Tom watches her as she stops, looks round again. She's looking round everywhere, at everything. Tom ducks further into the bushes as she looks in his direction. But she doesn't notice him. He watches through his covering of leaves as Jazz stands there thinking about something. He can see her making up her mind, turning round, going back up the road the way she's just come.

Weird, or what?

Tom watches Jazz disappear up the road. She's gone off in the wrong direction for school. Tom knows she isn't going again.

She's quite often not at school when she's supposed to be. Tom knows it. She's away too often for him not to have noticed. He doesn't say anything. He doesn't want to get anybody in trouble.

Except, of course, those Bainsies.

What Happened Last Night

But what about it? Last night.

I tell you what, mad.

Listen.

Tom was out with the Bainsies, those two twins who aren't even brothers, out scrumping down the big old house down the road on the corner, and guess who got caught?

Guess who was up the tree with the dumb Bainsies supposed to be on the look-out, when the Bride of Frankenstein flew out without touching the ground? Guess whose collar she grabbed off the tree? Guess where the brave Bainsies were by this time?

On their toes the pair of them weren't they, without a sound, gone, away, like the wind.

Tom felt his collar felt, looked round, no Bainsies. Looked round, the old mad woman, her big grey hair flying everywhere, her white gown blowing in the breeze. Looked round, her eyes – mad, or what?

I tell you. His collar tugged, he looked round, those eyes. Mad.

Tom was nearly cacking. He was breathing as if he'd forgotten how.

She was crazy, this old woman under her massive grey hair. She was off it, gone. Everyone talked about it. Nobody knew anything really. But they all talked. She was mad, for sure, that's what they all said.

So where do you think the Bainsies were, last night, when all this was happening to Tom?

But those Bainsies, eh? I mean, how can you be twins but not even brothers?

This is how.

Bainsey and Bainsey always wore exactly the same clothes. They had identical short spiky haircuts, identical wide-mouthed freckled faces both chewing gum in a kind of rehearsed unison. They were the same height, the same build. They said the same things in the same way, most of the time coming out with it at exactly the same moment. They laughed the same, in the same way, at the same time and at the same things. They were identical in every conceivable way. And they were both called Jimmy.

Jimmy Bains and Jimmy Bains were identical, but they were not twins. They were not even brothers. They went round telling everybody they were, but they weren't.

They were cousins. Their fathers were identical twins. Their fathers had got married at almost the same time, within a month of each other. They lived in the same street as each other. Their wives had given birth to baby boys within days of each other. If you'd have shuffled the boys, no one would have been able to tell whose was whose baby. They'd called them both Jimmy.

There were two Jimmy Bainsies, one exactly the same as the other.

The only difference between them was that one had a little red birthmark on his backside. So often, when they'd been babies playing in the park with their families, their mothers had had to remove their nappies to decide which one to take home.

After a few years, the parents could begin to tell the difference. Just about. But they had to look pretty closely.

Nobody else could tell. One Jimmy Bains was just exactly the same thing as the other.

Last night, those so-called twins were on their toes like a pair of whippets, leaving Tom face to face with the crazy lady nobody knew.

She was hoisting him by the scruff off her apple tree in her big garden. She was all grey hair and long white night-gown. Mad? You've never seen anything like it.

Tom got hoisted off the branch, the old crazy looking round to see if she can see Tom's mates. No chance. No way. They'd blown, first glimpse of her, not a word to Tom.

Tom didn't have a word for himself either. His mouth dried up, healed up. He was gasping. His collar was doing him in where she'd got a too-good hold of him.

He reckoned he was for it. He was going to get busted, nicked. Or else the old woman was about to do him in.

I mean, look at her.

Tom had by the scruff, Bainsies toed, mad woman mad and grey and blowing white in the breeze. Mad eyes.

Tom without any spit left in his head. Dead scary. Dead bad.

But the next thing Tom knew, he'd got a drink in one hand, a biscuit in the other, one in his mouth and a big bag of apples by his side.

Weird, or what?

Because you should have seen that old lady, who wasn't really so old, once you got past all that wild grey hair and got used to those eyes. She was weird, no way wasn't she, but she was good weird, funny weird, like, she was something else.

She was like a child. Climbing the tree with Tom she was, reaching out for the best apples.

She jumped out of the tree as if she could fly. She bet

Tom he couldn't jump from where he was. Tom looked down. No way.

'Bottle-job,' she said to him.

'You're mad,' Tom told her.

'And you're a wimp,' she went.

Weird, I tell you, how last night she caught him scrumping in her garden, how she looked like a nutter and acted like one, climbing up the tree to get the best apples. Weird how she ate them, sucking at the bite out of each one to get the juice, just like Tom did.

Weird how Tom found himself talking to her in her house, dunking a biscuit in his orange juice, because that's what she did, telling her about things. Telling her about things at home, about the family. About the way they were always having a go at him about something or the other. Always trying to get him to care about things he couldn't care less about. Like putting stuff in one place and not in another because it was supposed to go there. Who says so, Tom asked her, the mad woman.

'Who says stuff's supposed to go in one place and not in another?' he asked her. 'What difference does it make?'

'Beats me,' she told him, slupping up another orange-soaked biscuit.

Tom believed her too. You only had to have a look round her house. You knew she didn't get it any more than Tom did. Stuff was everywhere. All kinds of stuff. Books, thousands of them, in piles, piled up on top of other things, falling over all the big heavy furniture. Clothes and tea towels and towels were piled up, papers, magazines, strange wooden boxes, ornaments, branches from trees, seashells, pictures on the walls, off the walls, pictures of people in silhouette painted on the wall itself, lights in weird places, candles, old oil lamps, rugs, screwed-up letters and papers and ancient typewriters and a brand new PC and a snake on the desk.

What?

Tom noticed it now. A snake. A real snake in a massive birdcage on a hook over the desk with the computer turned on, and the snake's eye still and black as a hard bead.

'Fantastic!' Tom declared, going over to take a closer look.

'Isn't he?' she said.

'What kind is he?' Tom wanted to know.

'An Indian python.'

'Oh – fantastic. Is he tame?'

'Tame? You don't ever tame a creature like this,' she told him, but taking the python out of its cage. 'Isn't he beautiful?'

Tom was in a rapture, his mouth open, watching as the snake stretched its four feet or so of body up her arm, as its double black tongue flicked in the air, once, twice, three times.

'But you said it wasn't tame,' Tom said.

'You think he's tame do you? You come back on Saturday when he sees a rat. Then you tell me if you think he's tame.'

Tom watched the thing. He didn't think it was tame. He thought it was weird, to be looking into the eye of a snake.

It didn't blink. It never blinked. Ever. Never in its life can it blink, never even close its eyes to go to sleep. It didn't have any eyelids to close. It just gazed, so still, so very still, its black bead of an eye giving nothing away.

It was the most fascinating stare, hard, and fast, relentless, impenetrable.

'They hypnotise you,' Tom said, 'don't they?'

'No,' she told him, 'they don't. But you can see how sometimes people have thought they could. Would you like to hold him?'

'It's not even slimy,' Tom said.

'No snakes are slimy. They're beautifully dry and warm, aren't they?'

'It's the best. The most brilliant creature there is.'

'I agree. It breaks my heart to have to keep him here like this.'

'Why? How should you keep them?'

'You shouldn't keep them. They should be wild, where they belong, hunting, really living, doing all the things wild animals do.'

'Why do you keep him here then?'

'What else can I do? He was given to me by someone that couldn't keep him. They thought they could. They shouldn't try. Now I have to look after him.'

'Why didn't you take him to a zoo? They'd look after him.'

She looked startled at this, glancing at Tom from the corner of her eye. 'Because I hate zoos,' she said. 'Zoos shouldn't even exist. I'd rather keep him here.'

Tom shrugged. 'And feed him on live rats?' he said.

'And feed him on live rats.'

'Brilliant,' Tom said. 'I can't wait.'

Friday

Tom's down the road still, still looking for those Bainsies. But he has to get going, or he'll be late for school himself.

He reckons the Bainsies are probably hiding somewhere, scared witless they'll get put away for breaking and entering the mad woman's property.

Or they'll be quaking, reckoning she might have done Tom in or something. Because, when you come to think of how she floated out of the house dead silent as a daytime ghost, you'd not be surprised if they found Tom's body somewhere drained of all its blood. Just two puncture bitemarks on the side of his neck, other than that, sucked dry.

Tom toys with the idea of staying away from school for the day, to really put the squits up the Jimmy Bainsies. But then he remembers that the Bainsies hadn't come down the road, so they probably aren't going to be at school themselves. Besides, Tom doesn't do that bunking off school stuff, not like some of the others. What, was his name Jazz or something?

So Tom's away up the road to school without having set eyes on a single Bains. Not even half a Bains. Well, a single Bains is only half a Bains. Together they aren't any more than a single boy should be. Apart, they're both like the back end of a worm, squirming, no way to go.

But when Tom makes the playground, just before school starts, they're already there, the two halves of the worm, squirming. Only now they have direction. They know which way they want to go.

Tom spots them way over the other side. He's just about to go over, start having a go at them, start letting a few people know how they bottled out last night, how they'd legged it and left him up the tree. Tom was going to let everyone know what the Bainsies are really like, because that's what they deserve.

But then Tom notices the direction in which the Bainsies are squirming. They're making up to Whitbread, who's big. And dim. Oh, is Whit ever dim? Dim-Whit. But big. Oh, is Whit ever big? A big Dim-Whit.

But – is Dim-Whit ever nasty? Thick as a dozen sawn-off planks, nasty, completely humourless, greedy – is Dim-Whit ever greedy? Do Man. U. play football?

Dim-Whit – greedy, and nasty, or what?

Tom stops dead as he sees what the slimy Bainsies are up to.

Swinging off Dim-Whit's ear-holes they are, like a couple of matching ear-rings, one hanging off each lobe. There they hang, wheedling, whispering.

Tom stops as soon as he sees them there. He knows what they're up to. He knows exactly what they're whispering into Dim-Whit's deep dark head-holes.

Dim-Whit, he doesn't like Tom. Tom knows it. Well, Dim-Whit doesn't like anyone, but he hates Tom. Tom hates him too. He has done ever since Whit stuffed his head down the loo and pulled the chain on him. That's the sort of thing Whit does for fun, then doesn't like it if you hate him. Dim's maybe the dimmest person there is. Or ever was. If you don't make out you like him, he beats you up. So if he stuffed your head down the loo and pulled the chain on you, you had to pretend to think it was funny. Everybody else thought it was funny. Because it was funny if it wasn't happening to you.

But Tom hadn't thought it was funny. 'Get a heart attack fat pig,' he'd said to Dim-Whit when Dim finally let him up dripping.

'What d'you say?' Dim said, turning nasty.

'I said you're a fat slob and a moron,' Tom said. Then he'd ran like a whippet out of the loos and away across the playground and across the playing field before Whit could get his pork-pie hands round his throat.

Dim-Whit doesn't like Tom Rattigan. Dim-Whit doesn't like anybody really, neither does anybody like him. He's always starting on someone for something. He's always taking things off people, kind of forcing them to make a gift of their money or their grub. Either way, it all disappears into Whit's side-of-pork belly.

The girls hate him. His all-day blowing off. His nose-picking. He'd twist their arms if they said anything. He'd twist anybody's arm if they said anything. Anything. Dim-Whit doesn't care. He always feels good if people are hurt or crying. Especially if they're crying. You can see it on him, how much he likes it, how much it makes him feel powerful and special.

Oh, is Dim-Whit ever special?

Tom always knew that his turn would come round again. Whit only needed an excuse, that was all. Any old excuse would do.

Now here are the Bainsies like boy-devils, leaning against Dim-Whit's fat flanks whispering at Whit a reason to give Tom a good hiding. Tom can see the looks he's getting from there. He knows what's going on.

The trouble is, he can see from Whit's dim face it's too late to try and do anything about it.

The trouble is, Tom can see Whit's already seen him. Whit's already convinced he's got a good enough reason to splatter Tom's nose across his face, Tom can see it. He can nearly feel it as Whit starts over towards him, a smirking Bains on either shoulder. 'What do you want?' Tom asks of Dim-Whit as that big dumb tub looms large over him.

'I want you Ratty,' Whit goes.

The Bainsies are in the background now, laughing but nervous, rabbit-scared, nearly piddling with excitement.

'Leave me alone,' Tom goes, as Dim-Whit towers over him and round him like a side of mad-cow beef. 'Just you leave me alone.'

What Happened Last Night

'It's like this,' Tom said, last night, as they sat by the desk with their orange juice and biscuits, watching the snake.

The snake's tongue flickered, licking the air.

'It's like this,' Tom said. Then he told her all about it.

Weird, or what? Because, he'd never said all this to anybody else, ever. Not even to himself.

'The trouble is,' Tom told her, as the snake licked the air of entirely another world.

Tom was hypnotised, he reckoned. Why else would he bother telling the woman what the trouble was? Why would he bother telling her about the old man, always on at him to be like everyone else, his mum, always on at everyone because she's always trying to give up smoking? She was always smoking, always on about her nerves, how Tom and his dad were so good at getting on them, how tired she was at always having to clear up after everyone. Then Jazz, allowed to get away with murder because of the hormones she's supposed to have got.

'Home?' he told the mad woman, 'Mad, or what?'

Because it was always someone getting at someone else. Always someone going into one about something or the other.

Then school. Either it was Geography, or Maths, or something else he didn't want to do. Or else it was drawing things he didn't want to draw in Art, writing about things he didn't want to write about in English, or playing games he didn't want to play in Games. Like cricket. Like running. Like, was there any point?

Tom wanted to play football. He wanted to do football in Art, write about football in English, work out scores and that in Maths. Instead, instead, what did he get?

He got teachers. Teachers like parents he got, always going into one about something or the other, always wanting him to be like someone else, or at least not like himself. No one wanted to just let him be. They all wanted something else.

But Tom wasn't something else. Tom was just Tom. If they wanted something else they ought to just go and talk to someone else and leave him alone.

'They never leave you alone,' he told her, as the python curled itself round and round a branch.

'Is that what you want?' she asked him.

'That's all I want sometimes,' Tom told her. He leaned forward, running his finger down the bars of the snake's cage.

'Sometimes,' he told her, 'all I want is for them all to

go away, the whole lot of them. Just go away and leave me alone.'

He stared into the snake's cage.

'Wouldn't it be something,' he said, 'to be like the snake. I mean, not have any worries, no one having a go at you all the time about everything. Wouldn't it be nice not to have to go to school every day, not to have to get up when you didn't want to, not to have to go to bed when you didn't want to, or go to the dentist or anything like that?

Wouldn't it be great not to have to bother about anyone, the way the snake doesn't bother about anyone? Wouldn't it be great to have no one having a go at you?'

Friday

'What you want to have a go at me for?' Tom's asking big beefcake Whit.

Whit's coming for him. He's got that nearly smiling, thick and nasty face he uses when he's just about to hurt someone.

Tom knew this was coming. It was bound to happen some day. This day had been with him for months, ever since that other time, like a hard and indigestible pip in his stomach. He'd felt it there every time he'd seen the Dim-Whit. But he'd hoped, you know how you do, that it wouldn't have to come to this.

It wouldn't have either, if not for those Bainsies hopping and squirming there and calling all the other kids round to watch the fight.

Tom doesn't want to fight. Not with Whitbread

—— 22 ——

anyway. Whit's three times his size, easily. Whit is dim, and nasty, and doesn't know when to stop. Whit hurt some boy in the third year so badly a while ago, the boy had to go to hospital to have his eye seen to.

But somehow Whit never got into trouble for any of these things. It seems as if even the teachers, even the police are afraid of him.

'What you want to have a go at me for?' Tom asks him.

'You been having a go at my mates,' Dim says.

The mates he's referring to are those two spiky near-twins shaking and laughing at Tom from safety over there. Dim-Whit thinks those two are his mates. That's how dim Whit is.

'And you been mouthing off about me,' goes Whit.

'I haven't,' Tom says.

'No? Then how come all my mates reckon you have, eh?'

'All your mates? You haven't got any mates,' Tom says, before he can stop himself.

'You what?' goes Whit, lunging for him.

Tom darts out of the way. He's about to run for it, but there's a good bit of a crowd gathering round by this time going, 'Fight! Fight! Fight!'

Tom goes to leg it out of the way of big dim Whit, but what does he run straight into but the wall of kids all jostling and shouting and braying for blood. Tom's blood.

Tom's having none of it.

He turns round as big Whit's running for him and lands Whit with one hell of a boot right in the groin.

Whit's like one of those lumbering great dinosaurs with only a pea-brain in a big dense body, so he has to stop and wonder what's hit him for about nearly half an hour before he realises what it is and then he's in great agony.

He kind of stops dead mid-run, mid-grab for Tom's scruff, kind of just stays there looking dead puzzled and dead stupid. Well, Whit always looks dead stupid, but now he looks, looking puzzled, about a thousand times more stupid.

Tom's looking up at him, beginning to wonder if the volley to the groin's going to do anything at all, when Whit, almost as if he's only just remembered pain, lets out this animal great roar.

The ring of kids are quietened by the noise of Dim-Whit's pain. They're all shocked into shutting up, into a unanimous dead seriousness.

Tom watches in wonder as the great shout comes out to quieten the crowd, as Whit thumps down on his knees clutching his groin, flops to one side, falling in a faint like a fat flop piglet curled there on the surface of the playground.

The crowd separates as Tom turns, as he looks at them. The Bainsies, their traps hanging open, step aside, one to each side of the gap that's opening to let Tom through. The silent crowd parts like the Red Sea for Moses as Tom the Great and Giant-Slayer strides through. He steps on through, head up, chest out.

He has these visions, these instant dreams of people looking at him as he strides along like a wolf. 'That's the boy that downed Dim-Whit with one blow,' they're bound to say.

But he's dreaming. Tom's a dreamer. He's always getting into trouble for it. As he nearly is now.

As he's wolf-walking through the parted halves of the

sea of onlookers, a sound from behind him, the touch of a heavy hand on his back.

Looking back, big Whit's hobbling white-faced after him through the crowd.

Whit's nearly got hold of him by the shoulder. If Whit wasn't so dumb-heavy and clumsy, he'd have Tom in his clutches by now.

Tom leaps out of the way.

Whit lunges after him. 'I'm gonna—' Whit's gasping. 'I'm gonna – murder you, Ratty! I'm gonna – murder you!'

But Tom Rattigan's off down the corridor of the parted crowd, out the other side with Dim-Whit's mad shouting still promising murder on his shoulder. Across the playground he scuttles, Tom Rattigan, his wolf-walking dreams all suddenly evaporated. He scuttles like a rat, Tom Ratty, over and across the playground, not stopping, not looking back, out of the school gates, down the road, round the corner and gone. Well away.

He runs down the high street, ratty Tom, to the shops. He's clipping along on rat-claws trying not to get himself seen by anyone who might notice him away from school at this time of day.

Last night, Tom reckons, as he hangs about, trying to keep out of harm's way, it was weird, last night, really weird, but dead good. The snake, that house, the weird furniture, all big and dusty, the strange pictures and books everywhere, the cushions, the way nothing was put away. That's the way to live, Tom reckons. That's the way he's going to live, one day.

One day, when he gets out of this day, this trouble he's in. Because he is in trouble, every way. Big thick Whit's gunning for his blood. And Whit doesn't know when to stop. Tom has to stop thinking about that boy who had to go to hospital to have his eye seen to after Dim-Whit had got through with him.

Then school. He'd been seen, by any number of teachers from the staffroom window, he knows it. That's why they have the staffroom there, so they can look out of the window to see who's coming and who's going.

Tom's going to be in trouble at school. Which means big trouble at home. The old man goes berserk whenever there's any trouble at school. He'll be up there, trying to sort it out, but making things worse.

You don't – you just don't get your mum and dad involved in these things. It's like death for your reputation. You're as nothing when you're just someone that goes running to your mum and dad to sort your trouble for you. You have to sort it yourself.

Tom shudders remembering that boy's bandaged eye when he came back from the hospital.

But you have to face these things. It's horrible, depressing, but they don't give you the choice. There is no choice.

Tom had to run away today at school, and this is Friday, so no more school until Monday. But Monday's there, as sure as Tom's hungry now, through having hung about for hours down at the shops trying to keep out of the way.

No keeping out of the way of Monday though. And there's no avoiding this hunger growing in his belly.

He's got no money on him. He has looked, searched to the bottom of his school-bag. Not so much as a penny. Not so much as half a biscuit.

He looks into a shop, past all the packets of food to a clock on the wall. Half-past ten.

Half-ten and he's starved half to death.

What day is it? Friday?

Which day does his mum go to work?

Yes!

OK, let's go.

We go, Tom leading the way, back past the bushes where he'd waited for those Bainsies – yes, you wait till he catches up with that pair of haircuts. He'll have their guts.

His guts contract as he thinks suddenly of Dim-Whit having his guts. Suddenly, not only is he starving, but he wants the loo. He wants the loo more than he wants to eat. He starts to run. He runs up the road he watched his sister Jazz go back up this morning. He runs until he doesn't want to go to the loo any more. The hunger, and now a thirst, take back over.

Now he can see the house.

Good, no one's about.

He goes round the side of the house, in the back door. The back door opens. It's always left open. Tom stands in the back doorway listening for a few moments.

Nothing. Good.

In he goes. Fridge, orange juice. Straight out of the carton. Cupboard, chocolate digestives, two at a time. Orange juice, chocolate digestives. All right, now you're talking.

But just as he's starting to feel a bit better, a bit more like his old self, Tom hears a sound.

A sound he hears, just as he's about to crunch into another double digestive.

Someone's upstairs.

The parents are both supposed to be at work. Tom

saw them preparing themselves for work this morning. Jazz is at—

But Jazz isn't at school, is she? Tom had seen her turn round, make her way back up the road.

He puts down the orange carton and the double biscuits, opens the door, goes to the bottom of the stairs.

The bathroom door is closed.

There isn't a sound.

Not a sound.

Maybe Tom's imagining things?

He feels guilty, playing truant, running away from trouble. He feels bad. He likes school, in a way. In a way, he hates it. It always makes him feel as if he wants to go back on the loo every morning when he thinks about school. But there are some good mates at school, some good games of football, some right good laughs.

But just as Tom's about to turn back to his biscuits and orange juice, a sound stops him. A terrible, retching sound is coming from upstairs in the bathroom.

The sound of Jazz being sick makes the hair on the back of Tom's neck stand on end. He turns back. Jazz is being sick, really throwing up like crazy.

Tom waits at the bottom of the stairs until it all goes quiet again. But Jazz doesn't come out.

Tom waits.

Jazz doesn't come out.

Instead, another bout of retching, coughing and spitting into the bowl.

Tom treads lightly as he makes his way up the stairs. The noise continues from the other side of the bathroom door.

Tom reaches out for the bathroom door. As he does, Jazz goes quiet. Tom's hand freezes in mid-air. His heart's thumping. All the little hairs on the back of his neck are standing on end again. He cannot bring himself to open the door on her.

Instead, he creeps along the landing to Jazz's bedroom. The door of her bedroom isn't closed properly.

Tom's hand reaches out, slowly pushes the door of Jazz's bedroom. He just pushes the door slightly, it swings slowly aside.

Tom stands in the doorway of his sister's bedroom looking at the surface of her bed. He doesn't know what to make of it.

As he stands there, the horrible retching starts back up.

All over the bed, the wrappers of chocolate bars. All sorts of chocolate bars. Every type you can think of, Tom's looking at the empty wrappers. Dozens of them. All empty, all screwed into little balls, all scattered over the bed and fallen on to the floor either side.

Dozens of them.

The retching continues in the bathroom, on and on. On and on it goes as Tom finally turns from his sister's bedroom door back to the bathroom.

The terrible retching continues as Tom's hand goes out again, turns the handle of the bathroom door.

Jazz can't hear the door opening. Her head's half-way down the bowl, and she's still hawking and coughing and spitting.

Tom stands in the bathroom doorway watching his sister.

There's a strong, nauseating stench of chocolate and vomit. It all smells too strong, too sickly-sweet.

'What you doing?' Tom says.

Jazz turns her head violently, looking up with violent

hatred in her eyes. There's chocolate round her mouth, dribbles of chocolate-vomit dropping off her chin.

'Get out!' she screams.

'But—' Tom goes.

But Jazz is up, milk-chocolate white, covered in sick and sweat, spitting and sweaty and thin, but with her dangerous finger-nails clawing against the air in front of Tom's face.

'Get lost you moron!' Jazz screams. 'Get out! Get out!'

She's coming at him like more of a nutter than the crazy woman from last night.

Tom turns and runs down the stairs.

He feels sick himself from the sight and smell of it all. He doesn't understand what's going on.

Jazz is screaming, crying, gagging.

Tom's afraid. More afraid than when Dim-Whit was after him. This is serious. Too serious. Tom doesn't know how to handle it.

So he runs away again.

He runs out of the house and down the road. He can hardly breathe. He can hardly think. But somehow he knows where he's going.

He's going to the only place there is now to go. And he can't wait to get there.

PART TWO

Saturday and What Happened Last Night

Saturday

Saturday morning, mad, or what?

You get half a chance to get a decent lie-in for a change, what happens?

Up she comes, fag on, Saturday morning hair like nicotine, coming piping into the bedroom with the vacuum cleaner going and your dirty clothes flying and spray polish going *shshsh, shshsh, shshsh* all over your best dust.

'Come on you,' she's going, Mother of a Saturday before lunch, manic Martha smoking too much and blaming everyone else for the fact that she can't give up the fags no matter how hard she tries.

'Come on then,' says she, flicking fag ash on his carpet, picking it up with the vac. Then she's looking round for somewhere to stub the thing out. She hates smoking, she really does. She's always giving it up. Trying.

The old man gave it up, a few years ago. He's never let her forget that. 'I gave it up, why can't you?' He's always on at her for it. He's always on at her for something or the other. She's always on at him for something or the other. They're both always on at Tom for everything and the other, the pair of them pecking like vultures at Tom and at each other.

Jazz is the only one. She's let off. It doesn't matter what it is, there's always a reason why Jazz is let off. Hormones. The fact that she's female.

The fact that she's female! That's sexual discrimination. It is! Tom's always saying so. But all he gets for it is a knock round the side of the head and the advice just to do as he's told.

Do as you're told. Good, sound advice. Except that what he's told to do is always unfair, unnecessary, or just plain stupid.

Then she's yacking on, telling Tom he ought to grow up, then she's going all watery over some forgotten photo of Tom and Jazz when they were little on holiday.

She's one minute going on at Jazz for kind of idolising the posers in the boy-bands, next minute she's nearly fainting over some ancient actor in some ancient no-action film.

That's why she's so off it, because she's one thing one minute, the next, she's something else. And she is something else. What?

Like now, going berserk in Tom's bedroom, trying to get rid of Tom's decent bedroom stink by spraying everything with slime and violet-sick in a can. Nothing smells worse than Tom's room when she's been in there sloshing and spraying and sticking stuff everywhere it doesn't belong.

Tom wants to just dive under the cover till she's gone, but something's happening to him. What's happening to him? Remember all those apples from last night?

What Happened Last Night

He had to wait outside, wait in the garden, eating apples straight off the tree. Green, sour-sweet apples in September. The weather was still good, that was lucky.

Because Tom had to wait ages, hours in the garden eating green apples in the September sunshine waiting for the mad woman to turn up.

Tom had run from his house, down the road to the corner, tried to push open the big iron gates. They were locked. They were always locked.

Tom had scaled the wall again, as he had the night before with those Bainsies. Again the long drop down on the other side into the long grass. But this time Tom wasn't worried about being caught. In fact, he walked up to the front door of the big old mad house, knocked using the big black knocker. There was no bell.

He'd waited. He'd knocked again, waited. Nothing. No sign of life.

Tom reckoned she'd probably gone shopping or something, the mad woman, although he'd never seen her down at the shops. Before yesterday, he'd never seen her anywhere other than getting a glimpse of her like an insane ghost flitting through the overgrown garden in her overgrown night-gown.

So, he waited, bored with watching spiders fat and squat in the middle of their webs, bored with climbing for apples, bored with waiting and being bored. Being bored was so boring. Being bored was the most boring thing there was. But, when you had nowhere else to go, nothing else to do, it was back to catching flies, flicking them into the side of the web, watching the excited spider scuttle horrifically fast with its fanged poisonous mouth at the ready. Juicy.

'What, you again?' had come the voice from behind him as he attempted to look into a fat spider's mouth.

Tom had leapt up, the voice coming from behind him as it had, coming out of nowhere.

She had appeared, just appeared there, from thin air.

Tom felt all the little hairs on the back of his neck stand on end again.

She looked crazy, wild and windswept, mad with sleep like a hungry vampire. Like a horrifically hungry spider appearing on tangly, silent legs.

Tom leapt up. He thought he heard the crunch of a spider's jaws from somewhere beside him.

'Did I make you jump?' she asked him.

He felt like running, to tell you the truth. She looked different, more confused, more confusing than when he last saw her.

'What were you looking at?' she asked him.

Tom glanced down. 'Spiders,' he said.

'Spiders?'

Tom glanced down. 'There. Eating a fly.'

'Really? Where? Oh yes. Mmm. Tasty.'

They both watched the tasty meal being consumed for a few more moments.

'Some people think it's disgusting,' Tom said.

'What's disgusting?'

'Spiders eating flies.'

She shrugged. 'Things eat other things,' she said. But she looked so different, so confused.

Tom had to think twice about following her into the house. The thing is, she hadn't asked him to come in this time. She'd simply left the door open. Tom expected that this meant he should follow her in, but he wasn't entirely sure.

He stood outside for a few moments more, in the sunshine staring into the gloom of her cobweb house. He shuddered. Anything could happen to him in there.

'Has school finished already?' she asked him, giving him his share of the biscuits and orange juice.

'It has now,' Tom said. He'd just spent hours and hours in her garden waiting for her to climb out of her coffin.

Because she did, she definitely did, look like a vampire – her crazy hair, white skin, mad eyes.

Tom watched her eat some biscuit to be sure. He was pretty certain vampires couldn't eat biscuits, or drink orange juice. Blood only. But she dunked her chocolate digestive just like Tom did, licking her red vampire lips with a chocolate-orange tongue, just like Tom's.

Tom couldn't work out where the food could come from. After all, she never seemed to go out. Nobody ever saw her out anyway, unless she flew like a bat at night down to the corner late-night supermarket for blood-fresh liver and chocolate digestives and orange juice.

Tom noticed the snake on its branch in the cage, how its tongue licked the air for food, for blood.

'I wasn't expecting you back until tomorrow,' the wild woman said to him.

'I know,' Tom said, watching the snake.

'I don't feed him until tomorrow. You will come back, won't you?'

'I wouldn't miss it,' Tom said. 'Not for the world. But he's hungry now isn't he?' he said. 'His tongue's going like crazy. That means they're hungry, doesn't it?'

'Yes, it does. But they're best fed only once a week. In the wild, they'll feed more often, then less often, according to what food's available. But in captivity—'

'What do they eat in the wild?'

'Whatever they can catch. Mice, rats, birds, frogs. Small deer, some of the bigger ones.'

'What do you think we're supposed to eat in the wild?'

'Us? Human beings? I don't really know. All sorts. Depending on what's available. What do you think?'

'I don't know. Mars bars, chocolate éclairs, chocolate.'

'Wouldn't we all be sick?'

'Would we? Would we be sick?'

'Well we wouldn't be very healthy, not just on chocolate.'

'Yes, but would we be actually sick? You know, chucking up all over the place. Would we do that? Chocolate's food, isn't it?'

'Yes. Why do you ask?'

'Oh, I just wondered,' Tom said, concentrating on the snake.

Saturday

Remember Tom waiting in the garden for the wild woman to appear, eating little sour-sweet green apples one after the other?

Well, they're having their effect on Tom this Saturday morning. All of a sudden, with the vacuum cleaner going, spray-slime fizzing all round him, he has to sit up with a jolt.

His mother looks at him, wondering what's happened all of a sudden. All of a sudden, without another word, Tom has to leap out of bed, do a record sprint to the bathroom. Once those apples work, they work good. Real good.

He makes it to the bathroom, just. He sits there, trying to get some peace and quiet. But there she is again, that woman after him, knocking on the door, telling him to be sure to have a shower.

Tom's in and out of the shower in a minute, being as hungry as he now is. He's going to have one of his mega-mixes, four or five different types of cereal just about filling up a fruit bowl.

He can hear his mum having a go at Jazz as he's digging into his giant bowlful. She's on at Jazz to have some breakfast too.

Jazz is moaning. She doesn't want breakfast. She's not hungry, she insists.

But their mum insists she goes and gets something to eat. 'You don't have time for breakfast during the week,' Tom can hear his mum saying, 'and I can hardly ever get you to eat dinner. Go and make up for it now. Go on.'

'I don't want any breakfast,' Tom hears Jazz complaining.

'I don't care,' he hears his mother snap back, 'you do as you're told. You need your breakfast this morning. I'll be out at lunch-time, I want to be sure you have something at least.'

'But—' Tom hears Jazz try to say.

'No buts. Go and get your breakfast now. Now!'

Tom can hear all that. He can hear the long, long silence before Jazz decides to move herself.

Tom can hear Jazz coming down the stairs. He can hear, he can *feel* the reluctance in her faint, pale step.

Tom's sitting over his big mixture bowl of breakfast

cereal as Jazz slowly takes a small bowl from the cupboard. Tom's breakfast is a mash of wheat and corn and rice and raisins and sugar and chocolate and milk, while Jazz's consists of the few cornflakes she allows to drop into the bottom of her bowl, the short splash of skimmed milk she drips on to the top.

Tom takes another giant spoonful of everything, crams it all into his mouth. The point is, you have to have a bit of everything every time when you're having a decent mixture for breakfast, otherwise there's no point. Tom always makes sure the spoon's got all five types of cereal on it, every time. It takes a bit of cramming to get it all in your mouth at once, but in it goes.

His cheeks are bulging. He thinks maybe he's overdone it a bit because he can hardly swallow. A bit too dry it all is. So he tries to take a mouthful of orange juice. But there's no room for it and it runs out of the sides of his mouth and drips off his chin. No problem, because he can just gather the dripping orange into the mixture in his bowl.

Then he notices Jazz.

She's watching him with a kind of horror of disgust written all over her turned-up face. 'You're repulsive,' she tells him.

He'd give her a mouthful back, would Tom, if he didn't have such a mouthful going at the moment. All he can do is to chomp away and get some swallowing done as best he can.

He watches Jazz as she sits at right-angles to him at the table. Tom keeps glancing at her out of the corner of his eye.

There's hardly anything in her bowl to begin with. A few flakes, a dab of thin milk, no orange in her glass, no glass. She's sitting there glancing at Tom's great chocolate-brown bowl bulging with stuff, and she's swallowing nothing. But she is swallowing. Swallowing and swallowing she is, with no food having passed her lips.

'You tell anyone,' Jazz tells him, 'and I'll do you.'

She tells him this as she throws her few cornflakes into the bin, covers them up with waste tissue paper.

Tom has watched her watching him eat. He's seen the distaste and the illness on her face. He's watched her swallowing and swallowing her own spit. He's seen how she's tried to keep her stomach in place. The food has approached her mouth, slowly approaching on a shaking spoon. Finally, Tom has seen his sister throw the spoon back down, stand up and take the bowl over to the bin, throw her breakfast away, cover up the evidence.

'You tell anyone,' she says, putting her bowl in with the rest of the washing-up, 'and I'll do you.'

'Why would I tell anyone?' Tom asks her. 'Why would I want to waste my time talking about you?'

'Look,' she says, coming closer to him. She looks far too pale, with dark rings round her eyes. She looks so bad it's a wonder that their parents have never noticed. But then, parents only ever notice the things they want to notice. Most of the time they're too busy going out or coming in or watching the news to notice if anything's actually going on.

Tom knows what's going on here, now. It's written in his sister's pale drawn face, the venom with which she spits her words at him.

'Look,' she spits, her dark-ringed eyes bulging out at him, 'you just keep away from me, right? You just keep right away, if you know what's good for you.'

'What's the matter with you two now?' their mother goes, coming in unexpectedly through the kitchen door as Jazz is bearing down on Tom, threatening him with her dark, bulging eyes.

Parents. Dim, or what?

Why don't they ever see what you want them to see? Why do they always have to notice everything that doesn't mean anything to anybody, and miss all the important stuff? Are they stupid, or what? Are they? Parents? Do they ever understand anything you're doing in school? Never. What did they do at school? Nothing? School must have been dead easy when they used to go, because nobody seems to have had to do anything.

Parents always get themselves wrapped up in all the things that don't, really don't matter. Like, have you ever heard them all going on about what they were doing when the American President Kennedy was killed? Who cares? Who cares?

But that's the sort of stuff they're wrapped up in, like bad shell-suits, and too-tight jeans, like worrying about what's in food, calories and that, and additives and stuff – then missing out on the really important things, like, for instance, a decent pair of trainers, a good football match, brown breakfast-cereal milk, and the fact that their daughter's ill.

Tom's learning how ill Jazz is. That's why he just sits there and takes it all off her when she's having a go at him for nothing. That's why he says nothing when their mum appears unexpectedly and dimly notices nothing.

Why can't she see, their mum, that Jazz has got bulimia nervosa. As soon as the wild woman had said the words last night, Tom knew it was that. Tom had told her, the wild woman, about Jazz being sick. Tom knew that Jazz had made herself be sick somehow. Tom knew what it was. He hadn't wanted to put the words to it, that was all.

What Happened Last Night

For a long while, nobody spoke. Tom could feel the wild woman watching him. He was aware of how dark the big house was, except for the light illuminating the snake's cage. You could feel the heat coming from the lamp, but everywhere else, a strange chill, as if it was already winter outside.

'I wasn't expecting to see you today, Tom,' the wild woman said, eventually.

'No, I know.'

'I didn't think you were coming back until tomorrow when we feed him,' she said, nodding towards the snake.

'No. I wasn't going to. But I needed to – there's something I needed to ask you.'

'Oh yes?'

'Yeah.'

Just then, the snake turned its head. It turned its head until it was, or seemed to be watching Tom head-on, its face directed straight at his. The black, unlidded eyes bulged out from the sides as the slick black tongue skittered out tasting Tom's air.

'What did you need to ask me Tom? Is something wrong?'

Tom paused, gazing back at the python.

'It's my sister,' he told the wild woman, as the snake licked the air after the taste of rat, or small antelope, however they all tasted.

'Your sister? Jasmine, isn't it?'

'Yeah. Jazz.'

'Ah. What about her?'

'There's something wrong with her.'

'Something wrong? In what way wrong?'

'It's something – she's, like, gone kind of – on her own.'

'On her own?'

'Yeah. Like, not going to school. Bunking off all the time. On her own.'

'Oh.'

'And she's, like, weird. Mum and Dad don't notice, but she's gone sort of – like as if she hates everything and everybody except her stupid music and that, like I told you, but even more. Like she really hates everything and everybody. That's why she bunks off school and goes home and pigs out on chocolate and stuff and makes herself sick.'

'She's sick? Have you seen her?'

'Yeah. Today.'

'Tell me what happened Tom.'

So Tom told her all about it. Except that he didn't tell her anything about Dim-Whit or any of that. He told her he'd been to the dentist's then home afterwards. He told her how he'd gone into the house without Jazz expecting him to be there. He told her about the masses and masses of chocolate wrappers, the terrible stink of sweet sick in the bathroom.

The wild woman was leaning against the side of her desk in her white gown, watching him. She was thinking about what he was saying, but thinking so hard you could almost see it going on behind the creases in her forehead.

Tom got to the end of all he wanted to say. He didn't have anything else to tell her. He'd been through it all. But still she leaned there with her thinking face on in silence just looking at him.

Tom glanced up at her. She didn't alter. Tom looked away.

'And?' she said, at last.

'And?'

'And what do you propose to do about it?'

'What can I do about it?'

'Lots of things.'

'Like what?'

'You could tell your parents, for a start.'

'No,' Tom told her, 'I couldn't. I couldn't do that. Jazz'd kill me. She'd kill me if she ever found out I've told you.'

'Then why tell me?'

The snake came down from its branch, slowly unwinding, making its way round the cage at the bottom, its tail following on with a thump a long while afterwards. Tom could see it wanted to find something. It wanted to kill something.

'I've got to tell someone,' Tom said.

'Why?'

Tom thought about it. He didn't seem to know why.

But then he did know why. He remembered that it wasn't so long since Jazz had been just about his best friend ever. Ever since they were really small, ever since Tom could remember, it was the two of them, together. They used to do the same things together, good things, before everything changed so suddenly.

Jazz had been a really good friend. You could have trusted Jazz then. Not now though. Now Jazz was much more like most of your so-called mates – always trying to intimidate you, always trying to get one over on you. Like those Bainsies. You couldn't trust them.

Oh, there were some good friends amongst all the mates and the school-mates and the acquaintances. Like Eggy Miles. John Miles, Tom's best mate, probably. Eggy because of the brilliantly smelly stinks he could always do in assembly. Really funny, especially when you weren't allowed to laugh.

Yeah, Eggy was all right. Tom would normally be out with Egg somewhere on a Friday after school, usually getting a game started down the park. But this Friday wasn't normal. No way was it.

Jazz was in trouble. She was still his sister – and still, somehow, a mate.

'Because,' he said, 'something's got to be done about it. Something's got to be done to help her.'

'And what should be done to help her?'

Tom shook his head. 'I don't know.'

'Well, who *can* help her?' she asked.

Tom looked at her wild white face. 'Only me I suppose,' he said. But I don't know what to do. She's changed so much. She used to be all right. Like – just, all right. She was easy. Good fun. Then she started to change. Her hormones Mum always says. Hormones, moods, tantrums. She doesn't like anything any more. She doesn't like anything or anybody.

'She hates me,' Tom told her.

The wild woman did nothing as Tom said it. She didn't try to stop him saying it. That was what was so different about her. She let you say the things you wanted to say, to say what was the truth without trying to get you to change it into what adults, parents, usually wanted to hear. That was what made parents so stupid – they thought that if they got you to say things differently to how you saw them, then those things would *be* different. Parents pulled the wool down over their own eyes to make themselves more comfortable. They watched the news from Bosnia and shook their heads, but didn't once bother looking round at their own battle-scarred lives.

Parents never knew anything about their own families. The signs were there for anyone to read, only the parents never bothered noticing them.

Just as they didn't bother reading the signs Jazz left for them in her mood swings, her tantrums, her refusal to eat with the rest of the family, the signs written all over her face, in her dark, sunken eyes.

'Bulimia nervosa,' the wild woman said. Tom already knew. But what he learned last night was how much he already knew. He knew everything. Tom had read all the signs everybody else had chosen to ignore. Tom learned last night just how all the pieces fitted together to form the one picture of the sickness his sister had. Tom knew it all. But he had to learn what to do with what he'd learned. He had to learn that if anybody was going to do anything about it, it was going to have to be him. There was no one else.

Parents? Stupid, or what?

What?

Saturday

'Your dad and I are going shopping,' their mum says. 'What are you going to do?'

'Nothing,' says Jazz.

'Well,' she goes, without really listening, 'don't make any mess doing it. And what about you Tom?'

'Me?'

'You're going out to play footie, aren't you?'

'Me?'

'Yes, you. Or is there anybody else in here called Tom I might be speaking to?'

'No. Not today. I've got it – it's – too late. You got me up too late.'

'Well that's your fault, not mine.'

'I know. United are playing Arsenal this afternoon. I don't want to miss the kick-off.'

'That isn't for hours yet, is it? – Where're you going to, miss? Hey! I'm talking to you.'

This, because Jazz was wandering away from the table in a trance, her usual state of mind.

'Jazz!' their mum shouts at her. Jazz snaps, as if she has suddenly woken up. 'Where do you think you're going?'

'To my room?'

'Oh no you're not. You do the washing up on Saturday mornings, remember?'

Jazz sighs, looking up at the ceiling. Tom notices how big and bulbous her eyes look. He watches his mother, who notices nothing. Nothing.

'Your father and I are going shopping this morning,' she's going, that woman who notices nothing. She's lighting up another cigarette, shaking out the match, throwing the dead match in the bin. She uses matches nowdays, instead of her lighter. She threw the lighter away last Christmas, because she was definitely, definitely giving up. She's been definitely giving it up for the past nine months.

'We're going shopping,' she's going, 'and you're doing the washing up, and Tom's drying. OK? Tom?'

Tom nods OK.

Jazz flounces back to the table, picks up a magazine.

'I don't want any mess,' their mum's saying, going out. 'And no arguing, the pair of you. – Aren't you ready yet?' she's shouting up the stairs after the old man.

'I don't know why we're going shopping,' goes their mum, coming back in, looking for handbag, car keys, all the usual, 'we've got no money to spend. More debt I suppose. Anybody seen the keys? Never mind, I've found them.

'Aren't you ready yet?' she's shrieking, as the toilet's heard to flush, as the old man's running feet are heard coming down the stairs.

'Have you got the keys?' he's asking her.

'I've got the keys,' she's going.

'No mess you two,' he's going to the kids on the way out of the door, 'and no mess.'

The door slams behind them.

Suddenly it's quiet.

Suddenly it's very quiet.

Tom sits waiting for something to happen. But nothing happens.

Jazz stares at her magazine without reading any of it.

Tom waits for Jazz to say or do something.

Jazz does nothing.

Tom takes a wary look at his sister.

Jazz, feeling his eyes on her, tosses down her magazine, gets up, goes out.

Tom says to her, as she's on her way out, 'What about the washing up? Aren't you going to do it?'

Jazz stops, looks round at him. There's real hatred in her face.

Tom doesn't know why there's real hatred in her face. 'Mum said you're to wash, I'm to wipe,' he tells her.

'You must be joking,' she spits at him, then leaves, goes upstairs, closes herself in her room.

Tom looks at the pile of washing up.

Somebody's got to do it.

But it takes ages, doesn't it, the washing up and the drying and the putting stuff away and everything. Tom even has a go at that saucepan, even with all the burnt-on black round the edges. Well, there's still a lot of black burnt on when he puts it away, but still, he's had a go. Not that it matters, because his mum puts it away with all the black still burnt on it herself, so no one's going to notice.

No one except the old man that is. He notices all that kind of stuff. That's exactly the kind of stuff he does notice. A bit of burnt black on the saucepan, your cupboards when they've got untidy. Isn't that what cupboards are for, taking all your untidy and bundling it away in one go? If that's not what cupboards are for, then what's the point of them? If you have to keep your cupboards tidy, then you might as well keep the stuff anywhere. If it's tidy, what's the point of putting it away?

But that's the old man for you. Mad.

Everyone's mad, that's the trouble. That's why the

wild woman in her big dark house and flying grey hair and flapping white gowns, that's why she seems so normal – not normal – so sane. The whole world's gone mad except for the nutters and Tom.

Maybe Tom's just a nutter, like the nutters? Maybe that's why everyone seems so crazy?

But then Tom hears Jazz come out of her bedroom and go into the bathroom. As well as wondering what she's going to do to herself in there, Tom realises that it's not him that's off his head. He's not the one that needs help.

He doesn't go round punching people and beating them up and chasing them out of school like big dim Dim-Whit.

He doesn't go round reckoning crazy things like teachers do. Like, in Maths, the teacher trying to tell you that if you take a minus number and multiply it by another minus, you get a plus. A plus from two minuses! How crazy can you get?

No, he's not the crazy one.

It's all gone quiet in the bathroom. Too quiet. Tom doesn't like to have to think of what Jazz might be doing to herself in there.

'Someone's got to help her,' he'd said to the wild woman last night. But she hadn't told him who, or what can be done, or how to do it. He was none the wiser.

But it's gone horribly, dreadfully quiet in their house. Tom stands at the bottom of the stairs trying to listen. There's nothing to hear. It's gone so dreadfully, horribly silent Tom thinks he can hear something. He doesn't know what it is, but it's a low humming sound, a background noise, the sound too much silence makes pressing right up against your ear-hole.

Tom has to sneak up the stairs to get closer to what he's trying to listen out for. Not that he knows what he's supposed to be listening out for. But he's listening out like mad, his ear nearly pressing against the bathroom door.

He can't hear a thing. Nothing. It's as if she isn't in there at all. But Tom knows she is.

His ear moves a little closer to the door, a little closer still, until the outside rim of his ear just touches the paintwork. Nothing.

Then everything.

Suddenly the door's flung open and Tom's left there with his ear flapping in the air and Jazz standing there staring at him. But can she ever stare. Those eyes of hers, they bulge and pop, her lips pressed tight, her white face whiter than ever.

'I thought I heard something,' she goes. 'What do you want?'

Tom has leapt back out of the way, his back pressing against the landing banisters. 'Nothing,' he's going, 'nothing. I just thought—'

'What!' Jazz is demanding, coming at him, eyes, pressed white lips and clicking razor finger-nails. 'What! What did you think?'

'I just thought – you know, the match is going to be starting in a few minutes. I just thought—'

'You what? Match? What match?'

'You know. United. United versus Arsenal. This afternoon. I thought you might like—'

'What, football?'

'I thought you might like – you know – some of the girls at school really like the players.'

'You moron. You moronic mindless – no, you were spying on me, weren't you?'

'No.'

'You were spying on me,' Jazz is advancing towards him, her lips screwed into a knot.

'You were! You were spying on me you little—' and she slaps him one, right across the face.

'Don't!' Tom shrieks at her.

'Don't you!' she shrieks back. 'Don't you ever dare spy on me you moronic little—' she's trying to slap him again and again round the face.

Tom shoves his way back down the stairs. He shoves her away, but she's after him, spitting, spitting insults, her dangerous nails clawing once across one of his cheeks.

They tumble down the stairs, Jazz tripping over Tom's heels. She falls against him. Tom lets her fall. His face is burning where she has slapped and scratched him.

Behind him somewhere as he fumbles to open the front door, Jazz has fallen down the last few stairs. She is still screaming, spitting insults after him as he throws open the door, runs for his life down the garden path, then down the street.

Tom runs down the street away from his sister's screaming, spitting, scratching tantrum. He runs away from Jazz as he always seems to be running away from trouble lately. He feels like a coward, but he runs. He runs and runs.

He knows where he's running to. There never seems to be anywhere else to go.

PART THREE

Sunday and What Happened Last Night

Sunday

Sunday morning. Mad? What?

Hungover parents, sister like death warmed up, only not so warm as all that.

First thing, people getting out of bed, going to the loo, getting a drink, especially the hungover couple, gagging from their too long visit to the club last night, doors slamming, people wishing things aren't as they are.

Tom, for instance, wishing this wasn't another Sunday, but still Saturday, with the game in front of him, but without the severe slapping from his sister. Tom, for instance, wishing he didn't have to hear the complaints of headaches etc. from the parental alcoholic stink-bin next door. Tom, wishing, for instance, his mum could just give up smoking and drinking too much on a Saturday night and not just talking about it. Tom, wishing that she and the old man, for instance, could find something they enjoyed doing together which didn't have to include the drink that made them moan all Sunday morning and sleep and snore and blow off the whole of every Sunday afternoon.

Tom, for instance, wishing he could find what Sunday had going for it, other than that it's a nothing day that always, always leads straight into Monday morning. Bang, Sunday goes into Monday, the worst day of the week for having to get your back off the mattress.

Tom, wishing like mad that this for instance Sunday wasn't going to lead him bang into the Monday morning he was going to have to face big Dim-Whit on his own.

Tom gets himself out of bed as quietly as possible. He could do without anyone having a go at him for waking them up too early.

He sneaks down the stairs, making as little noise as possible, leaving the Sunday morning paper hanging sad and silent out of the letter-box, quietly opening the kitchen door.

But as soon as the door's open, he sees her there. There she is, sitting there, but slumped forward, her head resting on the table-top amongst all the empty breakfast cereal packets and milk bottles.

The whole kitchen stinks of sour sick cream and chocolate gone off.

Something's really ill in here.

What Happened Last Night

He'd legged like crazy down the road, his face burning from having been slapped and scratched. Yesterday this was, running away from Jazz, but running to where he might still be able to catch the kick-off.

Not that it wasn't bad what Jazz had done to him. It was. But missing the match, what could possibly be worse? Man. U. versus Arsenal. No way did you miss that, no way. United were going to murder them. Then they were going to beat everyone else in the Premiership and win the double. No, the treble. They might as well take the Coca-Cola Cup while they were at it. Then Europe. Yes! Come on you Reds!

But first, the Arsenal. A good trouncing, this afternoon. Only fifteen minutes or so until kick-off.

And where was Tom?

Running down the road with his smacked and clawed face stinging and hot, that's where Tom was. He'd legged it like crazy down the road when he should have been in front of the box watching the preliminaries, big box of popcorn, sandwich, fresh orange still in the carton.

That wasn't where he was though, was it. Where he was, by ten minutes to kick-off, was kicking up the side of the tall garden wall of the house on the corner. He was over the wall and up to the door and knocking by nine minutes to.

He was knocking like a lunatic. Five minutes to kick-off, he was still there, knocking frantically and kicking, shouting through the letter-box, throwing handfuls of gravel up at the far upstairs window.

'Wake up!' he was shrieking through the letter-box.

Three minutes to go. Still he was knocking, thumping against the heavy wood of the door.

'Wake up! Wake up!'

One minute.

Tom turned away. Where else could he go?

Egg's house.

But the door opened behind him.

'At last,' he said, swinging back round.

'What's the matter?' she said, looking confused and crazy and riddled with sleep.

'Where's your TV?' he demanded, barging his way into the house.

'What TV?' she said.

'TV!' Tom told her. 'Your TV!'

But the crazy grey woman just stood there as if she was confused by the word.

'I don't have a TV,' she said.

Tom sagged, like a sack of rice spilt open. 'But,' he said, 'the match. United – Arsenal. Now. It's started. On Sky.'

'Sky?' she went, crazy as they come.

'Yeah. Sky. Sky Television.'

'Never heard of it,' she said.

Never heard of it! Mad, or what?

Tom was mad now as well, going out of his mind with knowing the match was happening, right now, but with him here, like this, going nearly as off his head as she was.

'Where are you going?' she asked him. 'Tom? Where are you going?'

'I'm going to Egg's – no I'm not. I've just remembered,' he said, having just remembered that Egg was out today, fishing with his dad.

Tom was going round and round in circles, his stomach in a squirm of knots.

'You must have a TV,' he told her, 'you must have!'

'I had one once,' she said, 'a long time ago. I didn't have a sky one though.'

Tom looked at her. 'But the match,' he said.

'What's happened to your face?' she asked him, noticing the scratch and red marks on his cheek.

'Nothing. I know – radio! Have you got a radio?'

'Ah, now, I can help you with that. Can you get a sky radio?' she said.

Tom stopped. He took a real good look at her. Yes, mad, totally out of it.

Then she showed him to this kind of long sideboard with slats down it. 'There it is,' she said.

Tom looked about. 'Where?'

—— 60 ——

'There,' she said, pointing to this piece of old rubbish furniture. 'Open the doors.'

Tom slid the slatted doors back. Inside, some stonking great thing with massive knobs and dials and all sorts of gadgets that must have been new sometime just before World War One.

'What's this?' Tom asked her.

'That's my radio,' she said. 'Haven't you ever seen a gramophone before?'

'How do you turn it on?' Tom asked, not knowing how to even approach the thing.

'Here,' she said, turning a dial.

The dial clicked, a light came on, nothing else happened.

'It's not working,' Tom said.

'Course it is,' she said, 'you've just got to wait for it to warm up.'

'Warm up?'

'Yes, warm up. You don't know very much about wirelesses do you.'

'Not much,' Tom said, as some small sound started to come out of the bit in the middle that was supposed to be a speaker.

Some horrible noise was building up now, just the sort of thing you'd expect to hear on an antique like this.

'Ah,' the nutty woman went, 'Wagner. Magnificent.'

'We want Five Live,' Tom said. 'How do you tune it in?'

'Here,' she said, flipping this huge great dial. A great red needle was juddering up and down the dial as the tuner moved between the stations.

'Let me have a go,' Tom said, taking hold of the dial. He chased the needle up and down. Wagner kept coming out of the speaker, some old opera a real radio wouldn't have even bothered picking up.

Then, suddenly, it dropped into tune. The commentary.

'A magnificent goal!' the commentator was screeching. You could hear him jumping up and down.

'A goal,' the loony woman said.

'I know,' Tom was going, jumping up and down himself, 'but who for? Who for?'

'How does he do it?' the jumping-up-and-down commentator was going.

'Who?' Tom was going back.

'The goalkeeper certainly doesn't know,' the radio voice said. 'A magnificent goal from the Arsenal striker. A goal from nowhere.'

'Oh no,' Tom said.

'Isn't that any good then?' the lunatic with no telly asked Tom.

'Any good? Any good? They're losing. United are losing to Arsenal. Does that sound any good to you?'

'It does if you like Arsenal,' she said.

Tom looked at her suspiciously. 'You're not a Gooner or anything, are you?'

'I don't think so,' she said.

But Tom didn't like it. She didn't think she was a Gooner, but she didn't actually know. And Tom doesn't like Gooners. Dim-Whit's a Gooner, and Tom hates Whit, you know that.

In the end though, she wasn't. A Gooner that it. Mad, she was. Gooner, no. In fact, she didn't know the first thing about football. She kept thinking that offside meant they had to have a throw-in. Or a scrum, she said, at one time. A scrum!

'What planet are you on?' Tom asked her.

But, mad or not, she was all right. She supplied the chocolate biscuits and the orange, she kept quiet when she was supposed to keep quiet, and she jumped up and down and cheered when Tom did when United got the equaliser.

'Is it finished?' she said, after the full-time whistle.

Tom wasn't satisfied. He wanted the Gooners thrashed, not drawn with.

'At least they didn't lose,' she said.

'No,' Tom said, 'they didn't lose. Neither did Arsenal, that's the bad thing.'

'I see what you mean,' she said, crazy as they come. Crazy as that, because Tom looked as she said that and saw what she had.

What she had was a dirty great rat by the tail. The dirty great thing was squirming in the air being held there only by its string-thick tail.

Tom leapt up. 'What the—'

'It's time,' she went, crazy as they come.

'It's time the snake was fed,' she said, holding the rat in front of Tom's face, its eye glinting and looking straight into his own.

Sunday

Jazz's face is flattened against the table-top, a pool of spit gathered under the corner of her mouth.

Tom approaches her as if she's dead. She might be, judging from the colour of her. White she is, white as paper, her lips all sort of bluish and hard.

Death warmed up? Not nearly so warm as that.

Tom shivers as he gets closer to her.

That smell.

That horrible smell of dead milk and sweet, sickly, chocolaty yoghurt.

That smell, if nothing else, could make Tom think that his sister has died.

He turns, as if to run away, as if to fling the door back open and call out for his mum and dad, to scream to them for help.

But as he turns, he hears a noise.

Jazz lets out a little moan. A little, milk and saliva snore escapes from her.

Tom turns back. He creeps closer to her. Her head is almost completely surrounded by half-eaten cereal packets and empty milk-bottles and cartons.

Now Tom can hear his sister breathing. It's good that she is breathing, but now you can hear it too much, as if something is blocking its way.

She looks, she smells, she sounds sick.

Tom moves one of the bottles to get a better look at her.

As he moves it, Jazz's eyes blink open.

But the eyes are empty, glazed over, pale, bloodshot.

Tom steps back away from her. He's afraid of her. Who wouldn't be?

But her lips are moving.

Tom's afraid of her, but moves closer to hear what it is she's saying to him. He can't hear her. So he moves closer. He moves his ear close to her mouth, so close, the smell of sick on her makes Tom feel sick.

'What did you say?' he whispers to her.

— 64 —

He can hear her breathing more easily than he can hear her words.

'What did you say?'

'Please help me,' she's saying to him through her breath. 'Tom, please help me. Please, please help me.'

Her head looks as if it's fixed to the table-top, it's so heavy. She hasn't slept. Anybody could see. She's been up, eating, being sick, making herself sick, eating again. Being sick again.

Now here she is, half killed by herself, by the madness that's got into her somehow.

How?

Tom doesn't know.

For a few seconds, he doesn't know what to do. He very nearly calls for help from the hungover couple upstairs. He very nearly calls up the stairs for them to come down and take over. Tom doesn't feel up to dealing with it. Why should he?

But this is Jazz lying there, just lying there. Jazz, his best sister. His one-time best friend. And she needs his help.

Giving her up to the authorities isn't likely to help her. In fact, imagining the hysterical reaction of the parents, Tom knows that isn't the way.

He tries to pick her up. Dragging her arm round his shoulders, he hoists her. She's heavy. She's sick and thin, but she's a dead weight.

It's as if she's drunk. She breathes like a drunk, as if she's about to be sick.

'I'm going to be sick,' she splutters.

'No!' he tells her. 'No more sick. That's enough. Breathe properly. Come on, help yourself. Let's get you upstairs.'

They fumble, they stumble up the stairs, clumping and thumping and going two stairs up, one back.

They finally make it to the top of the stairs. They stop. Tom stops them. He listens. Good. No sound from their parents' room.

Tom's able to drag Jazz past, bundle her into her own room, heave her into bed.

She's heaved on to the bed, heaves down to be sick. She doesn't bring anything up now though. There's probably nothing left inside her.

'How do you get yourself like this?' Tom asks her.

She turns over, looking palely up at the ceiling. 'Once you start – being sick – you can't stop. You just – can't stop.'

'Well you're going to have to,' Tom tells her, leaving her there, closing the door on her. He stomps back down like someone who hasn't found his sister sick, slumped over the kitchen table.

He puts the big bowl Jazz has emptied of heaven knows how much breakfast cereal into the sink. He rinses the bowl, and the sink because it stinks of sour sick and chocolate milk regurgitated. He puts the washed bowl on to the drainer before starting to clear away all the empty and half-empty packets from the table.

His head is in the cupboard as he stuffs the last packet away, when a voice goes, 'What are you doing?' but from right next to him.

He leaps. Head bangs.

His mum looks worried. 'What are you up to Tom?'

'Nothing. I – nothing. Why?'

His mum's looking worriedly round the kitchen. You know mums, when they look worried, they look dead worried. 'I thought you were putting breakfast cereal away.'

'I was.'

'But you never put things away. And there's a bowl washed up on the side over there.'

'Yes. I washed my bowl up.'

His mum's nearly staggering by this time, you can imagine. Tom never puts anything away.

'You never put anything away,' she says to him. 'Washing up your breakfast bowl? What's going on Tom? What's happening?'

Tom shrugs it off. He goes out, his mum watching him, as if he's full up to the brim with breakfast cereal.

Then, later, of course Tom's ravenously hungry. He's told his mum there's nothing going on, but he's had his breakfast and decided to wash up and put the things away to help her. He hasn't had any breakfast of course, that's why he's so very hungry.

But she's looking at him whenever he reappears in the kitchen, looking at him as if something spooky's going on. It is, but Tom doesn't want his mum to know. She's already suspicious about the marks she saw on his face last night. She's looking at him as if he's acting very strangely. Which, of course, he is.

So Tom escapes as quickly as he can. He goes upstairs. He's ravenous. Tom loves his breakfast, doesn't he? But he's been denied it this Sunday morning, thanks to that sister of his. Tom's sister, mad? You know it.

He knows she'll be asleep now, sleeping off the sickness she's induced by pigging and retching, pigging and retching. Tom knows what these Bulimians do.

He also knows Jazz, as the good Bulimian she is, will have a drawer crammed full of milk chocolate bars.

Tom knows she'll be in a dead sleep.

Tom knows, he can feel with the watering of his mouth, the milk chocolate hidden under Jazz's knickers in the drawer.

He has to go for it. He's too hungry not to.

He pushes open his sister's bedroom door. He slips in. The door slips closed behind him.

She's there, almost exactly where he left her, lying on her back, her pale face up, brown eyelids drawn closed, her breath no more than a snake's breath.

Tom slips across to the chest of drawers on the other side of the bed. He bends closer. He sniffs. He can smell the chocolate in the bottom drawer, the knicker drawer. He smiles to himself.

He glances at Jazz as she lies there white as a vampire with a vampire's dark, sunken eyes.

One glance at his sister, he goes for it. He slips open the drawer. It opens, but not smoothly. The wood clicks, creaks like a coffin-lid.

One creak, the vampire eyes click open. Tom can hear the click of the eyelids opening. He freezes. He can hear the vampire-hiss of his sister, the creak of her fangs growing, the click of her talons snapping into place.

Tom flinches as she appears, a vampire beside him, her red eyes full of blood. 'No!' he says.

But Jazz is swaying, blinking. 'What?' she's going. 'What's the matter?'

'Nothing,' Tom tells her. 'I've had to miss my breakfast. I'm hungry.'

Jazz is looking into her drawer full of chocolate bars.

She's blinking as if she cannot believe what she's seeing in there.

'Can I have some?' Tom asks her.

He's watching her face. Tom never knows what she's likely to do next. She is so unpredictable nowdays. You just can't talk to her any more.

She's still blinking at the contents of the drawer as Tom waits for her to react. He's half waiting for her to go for him, as she nearly always does, shouting him down, slapping him, or, like yesterday, clawing at him.

But she's even more confused than usual. She's weaker, more tired. She's surprised by the sheer amount of chocolate she's managed to collect. It seems to be telling her how far she's come, how far down she's gone.

'Have it all,' Jazz says suddenly. Then she sinks back, falling back into bed. The effort of just getting up has worn her out entirely. She lies on her belly, her pale face turned to one side.

Tom looks at her as he unwraps and starts to eat his first bar. Jazz looks as if she might start to suck her thumb any moment now. She looks young, too young, like a little tiny child.

Tom stands looking at her, helping himself to more chocolate. The more he looks at his sister, the less he seems to recognise her. It's strange, how strange she looks.

'Jazz,' he says to her.

She doesn't move. She looks quite dead.

'Jazz.'

Nothing. No movement. Tom cannot detect that she's even breathing.

'Jazz,' he says, touching her arm.

Her eyes flicker open. She opens her mouth slightly. She mutters something, but it's nothing.

'Jazz,' Tom tells her, 'you're really, really sick. Do you know that?'

Jazz's mouth opens slightly. She lets out a moan. It isn't a word, just the wisp of a moan.

'Jazz,' Tom tells her, 'you're really sick, and I ought to tell Mum and Dad about it.'

Jazz's eyes snap open. She raises her head slightly, tries to stare at Tom. 'Don't you—' she manages to say.

'But I'm not going to,' Tom says.

Jazz lets herself go again, collapsing into her pillow.

'I'm not going to,' he tells her, 'if you agree to do one thing.'

Tom waits for Jazz to question what that one thing might be. He waits for her to do that, but she doesn't do anything. She looks dead again, or in a deep, dead sleep.

'Jazz?'

She's not there to answer him.

'Jazz,' he says again, reaching out to touch her arm.

She draws away at his touch, as if touching hurt her in some way. Her eyes open slightly.

'You've got to do one thing,' Tom says.

Jazz looks at him through only slightly opened eyes.

'Can you hear me?' he asks her.

She nods, slightly.

'You've got to come with me,' Tom tells her. 'Today. When you've had a sleep.'

But Jazz looks as if she's having a sleep now, her eyes have closed back down.

Tom gets hold of her by the shoulder. 'Listen to me,' he tells her, 'open your eyes. That's better. In a minute you can go to sleep. First you've got to agree to come with me.'

'Where?'

'To see someone.'

'Who?'

'Just someone. A lady. She can help you.'

'No she can't.'

'Look, don't worry about it. Just agree to come with me, will you? Will you?'

'What if I don't?'

'Then I'll have to tell Mum.'

'Then I'd better,' Jazz goes.

'Yes,' goes Tom, 'you'd better.'

What Happened Last Night

Eye to eye, the rat's glinted pinkly into Tom's.

What was going to happen to it? What would happen to its eyes, its teeth, the white fur, all its bits?

It dangled by its tail in the air in front of Tom's face, looking about as much like food to Tom as someone's cut toe-nails.

'It's time,' she said, crazy as they come.

'But – where did you get it?'

'The rat? I bought it.'

'But it's – it's white!'

'I know.'

'With pink eyes!'

'Yes, I know. It doesn't matter. The snake won't mind.'

Maybe. Maybe the snake wouldn't mind – but Tom

—— 71 ——

seemed to. He'd imagined a real rat – a black evil looking thing with evil black eyes. He'd imagined the mad woman catching evil black rats in her dark cellar. He'd imagined the snake devouring vermin, not this – this looked like a pet, a pretty white pet with a pale pink tail and pink-red eyes. This thing dangling there, it looked – it looked as if it didn't deserve to be eaten by some bully of a serpent. All of a sudden Tom felt very different about the whole thing. He suddenly wanted a way by which he could call it off. A way by which he could run away and forget this was happening, that dreadful things had to happen, that the undeserving were often the victim, sometimes bullied, sometimes, killed.

But the crazy woman, mad as they come, led the way to where the snake tasted rat on the air with his glistening tongue, his black, lidless eye glistening, no white fur on his hide, no shivering whiskers, only glistening beauty, and terrible, dangerous and beautiful brute strength.

The mad woman led the way, her white gown flouncing out behind her, her mad fly-away hair falling and flowing.

The rat made no movement. Its pink feet splayed showing its little white claws in the air.

Tom followed on, watching them approach the serpent's cage. He could see the hard and brilliant creature coiled there on the branch, its machine body too dead still, its computer eye collecting movement, changing the movement of their approach to the cage into something still, something deadly, inhumanly still.

Mad as they come, the wild woman reached out to the cage door. Tom stood silent as she clicked open the cage door, as the rat blinked and quivered.

Tom flinched as the snake's dead-still machine head instantly shifted to a new dead-still machine position, as its dual-tongue licked the new, rat-tasty air.

'No!' he cried out, Tom, before he knew what he was saying.

He'd stood there as the rat clung on to the cage bars with its little pink feet as if it knew what was in wait on the other side.

'No!' he cried out, unexpectedly.

Well, he hadn't expected to do it, neither had the mad woman expected him to. She nearly jumped out of her skin. She let go of the rat. The rat took its opportunity and jumped for it, landing with a little thump on the rug.

'What?' the mad woman went. 'What's the matter?' she went, as the rat took its leave, scuttling under a chair.

'Look now,' she said, watching the rat, 'it's getting away.'

Tom walked over and clicked the snake's cage closed.

'Go round the other side,' she went to him. 'Watch to see if it runs out that side.'

But Tom just stood there by the snake's cage watching the mad one rat-catching.

'Come on,' she told him. 'I'll never catch it on my own.'

'Don't frighten it,' she said, as Tom dived into a rattle and crash of table legs and walking-sticks and umbrellas, diving across the floor, skidding, turning, smashing into tables and sticks and brollies.

'Don't frighten it,' she said, dead crazy. Frighten it? The thing was scared out of its wits of being eaten whole by a snake! What could Tom possibly do to frighten it any more than that?

But the rat was away, scratching across the floorboards looking for a decent hiding place. Let's face it, there were enough there. So much furniture, old stuff, books, junk, walking-sticks, brollies, piddle-pots, newspapers – so many places for a rat with an allergy to being eaten alive to hide out.

'There it is!' the mad woman cried, floating on her flouncy clothes like a spectre between the furniture.

'There it goes!' she screeched, laughing like a lunatic.

Tom dived for it. He got a hand on it. The rat squealed and turned over, scratching Tom's hand.

'Ow!' he cried, pulling his hand away. 'Blow that for a game. Not me,' he said, getting up. 'No way.'

'Wimp,' the crazy lady said, sniffing the floor like a terrier. 'Let me show you how it's done,' she said, grabbing a straw waste basket, tipping out the mess of screwed up paper. Not that you could see where all the waste paper went, as all it did was get lost in all the waste paper already strewn about over the floor.

The rat could be heard scrabbling through the waste.

Tom stood back as the crazy woman followed the rat's scratching, as she threw the newspapers and screwed paper aside, bits flying everywhere, as she clumped the bin down over the rat as it ran for new cover.

Tom watched her get down on her knees, carefully lift the bin on one side, reach in her hand, bring the rat back up into the air by its tail.

Tom watched the rat raised, its twitching face and legs looking just as though nothing had happened.

Tom watched the rat approaching him. He watched the thing close, this close to his face as the mad one held it up almost to the tip of Tom's nose.

'There you are,' she said.

Tom nodded.

'Now,' she went, 'tell me – how's your sister?'

What? Mad, or what?

Tom nearly staggered back, he was so surprised to be asked like that, at that time. But, what can you expect but the unexpected from complete nutters like her?

'I think,' Tom said, 'I think – she's going – you know – she's losing it.'

'Losing it?'

'Yeah, off it.'

'Off it?'

'Yeah, off her head.'

'Oh. You think so?'

'Yeah.'

'You think she needs help? I do.'

'I know you do. So do I.'

'You'd better get her some then,' she said, nearly waving the rodent in Tom's face.

Tom's face was backing away from the little pink claws scrabbling by his nose. 'What do we do now?' Tom said, talking about the rat.

'We?' the nutty woman said. '*We* don't do anything. You do it. You get her some help. Some counselling.'

'No,' Tom said, 'I mean with him,' nodding at the rat in front of his nose.

'Him? It's a female.'

'Female? How can you tell?'

'It doesn't matter. A him or a her, it's all the same to the snake. It's all food.'

'I know. It just makes me – you know – I feel kind of—'

'Well,' she said, with the rat swinging slightly on its tail, 'everything's got to eat.'

'Yes,' said Tom.

'And,' she said, 'they've all got to eat the things they eat. Or else they don't. And we know what that means, don't we?'

Tom nodded.

They turned towards the snake's cage. The snake's skin glistened green and gold in the light. The snake's tongue glistened black.

Tom wondered what the air tasted like. And how the air tasted of rat. And how that could possibly taste any good.

But nothing happened. Still as death the python watched nothing apparently from its black, blank eye as the rat buried its head in the corner. The rat's haunches bunched up round it for protection, its tail stopped dead as a drowned worm.

The rat hid its eyes, afraid. Tom blinked, swallowed, horrified, shaking secretly, while the mad woman drooled over her curiosity. She, besides the snake, was the only one in that room that wanted it to actually happen. If you'd have put it to the vote, there would have been deadlock, two for, two against.

Tom was thinking, I wish things like this didn't have to happen. I wish, he was thinking, that the snake could eat carrots and that, seeds, like the rat does. I wish the rat wouldn't just do what it does, just waiting there for something terrible to happen.

I wish, Tom was thinking, things wouldn't just wait for something terrible to happen.

But nothing happened. Nothing went on happening and went on happening.

Sunday

'Tom!' the old man's shouting up at him. 'What are you doing up there?'

'Nothing,' he's shouting back down.

'Then come down. Don't you go waking your sister up. Let the poor little thing have a lie-in in peace, can't you?'

'Yeah,' Tom says to himself, but quietly, 'I can do that,' he says, because he's spent the whole morning just hanging round the house waiting for the poor little thing to wake up.

'I don't know what you're hanging about for so much today,' his old man goes to him as Tom comes down the stairs. 'You up to something or something, are you?'

So Tom has to hang round the house with the old man eyeing him suspiciously, with nothing decent on the telly and the old man burping off his hangover before lunch.

Tom's bored out of his skull, naturally. Sunday morning indoors, what did you expect? He's usually down the road by this time, long before this time, kicking a football over the park and—

'Why aren't you down the park kicking a football or something?' the old man wants to know. 'You not feeling well or something?'

'I'm all right,' Tom tells him.

They're sitting together in the living-room. His dad's trying to read the newspaper, but can't seem to concentrate with Tom there. That's why he keeps accusing Tom of things, of being up to something, of not feeling very well. Typical. Tom's dad never really talks to him. Tom's dad only ever wants to have a go at Tom about something, only ever wants to not have to be bothered by Tom, or by anything. He only ever wants to read the paper, or do a crossword, or fall asleep, or do his car, or have a go at Tom, never anything good, never anything worth doing. Waste of space, the old man, if you ask Tom.

Look at him. Look at him now, glancing at Tom round the side of the paper as if Tom really really got on is nerves just by being there. Just by sitting there doing nothing Tom really really gets on his nerves so that he can't concentrate on his paper. Tom could prevent the old man dozing off to sleep, just by looking at him.

Tom's mum's clattering in the kitchen, doing something cold for their lunch. The old man won't bother helping her. He'll just sit and wait. Waste of space.

But then they can hear the poor little thing's bedroom door open. Just after that they can hear the loo flushing.

Tom's mum appears from the kitchen. 'Is that Jazz up at last? About time.'

'Let the poor little thing have a lie-in,' the old man goes, repeating himself as usual, his face still hidden behind the newspaper. 'She's been looking a bit peaky lately.'

'I've noticed that,' Tom's mum agrees, without thinking too much about it.

Jazz appears in her rotten old dressing-gown, her hair like rat's tails, her bloodless face a patchwork of too dark and too pale.

'There you are,' their mother says to her.

Jazz ignores everybody, as she does.

'You're going to be too late for breakfast,' their

mother tells her, 'because it's very nearly time for your lunch.'

'I'm not—' Jazz starts to say.

But Tom pipes up, springing out of his chair. 'We're not staying for lunch,' he says.

The old man's paper lowers. Both Jazz and their mum look at Tom in surprise.

'No,' Tom goes, 'we're going – up the town, for a burger.'

'What?' their mum goes, aghast. 'What?'

'Yes,' Tom goes on, 'we're going for a burger. Together. Aren't we, Jazz?'

Jazz looks dark, confused. But she looks too tired, too withdrawn to be able to fight it. 'Yes,' she says. 'We're going for a burger.'

'Who's paying?' the old man wants to know.

'Jazz,' goes Tom. 'Aren't you, Jazz?'

Jazz nods, reluctantly.

What Happened Last Night

Then the glistening head moved.

It clicked from one position to another, just, suddenly, went. As if something had triggered it. The snake's glistening head moved, tilted, its black eyes dead set forward on to the floor of the cage.

Tom had been doing nothing.

The crazy woman, doing nothing.

The rat, nothing out of the ordinary. Scratching, that was all.

Then suddenly, quite, quite sickeningly of a sudden,

the glistening deadly beautiful head moved into another position. The new position told you. You could see that nothing was about to stop its happening. Something was going to happen in its place.

That stopped Tom from thinking about his sister.

That stopped the woman from thinking her crazy thoughts.

That stopped the rat. The rat shivered.

Tom shivered. He felt his pulse begin to race. He heard the mad woman take a little sharp breath in her excitement. He felt all the little hairs on the back of his neck stand up.

Then bang! The snake, faster than any living thing should be, was on it. Bang! And down, completely, and wrapped round and round the rat, so fast, so horribly fast.

'Oh no!' Tom uttered.

'Shshsh!' she hissed.

The snake's coils wrapped the poor white and pink creature closer, tighter, still tighter. Tom could see its mouth opening and closing, gagging for a breath of air. Its little mouth was opening and closing, gagging for its life.

'Still think the snake's tame?' the crazy woman whispered to Tom.

Tom reckoned no, no way was it tame. But he didn't say anything. He watched the rat. A tame rat, constricted until the air was all squeezed from its lungs. A pet, its mouth open, one loose straggly leg twitching the last of its life away.

Then he watched the snake loosen, its coils slacken, its head creep round to face the dead rat's dead snout. Tom watched the snake's mouth open over the rat's white face, that little white face disappear, the snake's head distort, its jaws dislocating as the rat's whole body disappeared a little at a time into that great opened mouth, the jaws now just a stretch of skin at the sides, the black eyes lifted, transported on to the top of the distorted head like a frog's.

Tom watched the massive, all-in-one swallow, the pet rodent now nothing but a lump in the throat and a tail like a pink mammal-hair tongue hanging from the tip of the snake's mouth.

Tom felt – he felt quite ill.

'What's the matter?' the lunatic woman said to him. 'Can't you take it? It's what happens. It's what must happen. Some things die, others live. It's what happens.'

'But who decides?' Tom wanted to know. 'Who decides what's going to live and what die?'

'We do!' the woman pronounced.

Tom looked at her. Suddenly he didn't want to be here. Suddenly she was too mad. Suddenly, everything looked too mad, and wild, and too desperate. Everything looked too hungry, too greedy, too selfish. Suddenly, everything looked as if it had all gone wrong, as if Tom was the only one left anywhere with any sympathy for anyone or anything. As if Tom was the only one left with an ounce of compassion.

'Bring her to see me,' the mad woman said. 'Bring your sister here.'

'Here?' Tom said, wanting not to be here himself. 'Here?'

'Why not?' she asked, shrugging. 'Where else have you got to take her?'

Tom looked at the lump in the snake's throat. 'I don't know,' he said. 'Nowhere I suppose.'

'Then bring her here,' the mad woman said. 'Bring her here.'

Sunday

'I'm not going for any burger,' Jazz is going, as they're going up the road. 'No way am I ever going to eat burgers. I wouldn't—'

'No,' Tom pipes up, 'but I would. And I am. And you're going with me. And you are paying for it as well, because I missed my breakfast thanks to you and I'm starving and I'm not going to miss my lunch, not for anyone. Right?'

Jazz doesn't bother saying anything.

'Then when I've finished, I'm taking you to see someone.'

Jazz jerks a stab of a look in Tom's direction.

'I'm taking you to see someone,' Tom tells her, 'and you're going to go.'

Jazz looks away. 'I tell you something,' she says.

'What's that?'

'I'm not going to sit there watching you eat that junk. I'm definitely not doing that.' So she waits outside for him while Tom eats. He takes his time. He doesn't care. As soon as he comes out, she's on at him.

'I don't know,' she's going, 'how you can possibly think that stuff tastes any good.'

Tom has eaten two big burgers, large fries, large shake. He doesn't care.

'I don't know how anybody can bear to put that stuff

in their mouth,' she's going to him, as they make their way up the road.

'It's better than eating nothing,' Tom tells her.

They make their way to the corner where the big house stands behind its walls and railings. Tom stops, looks through the railings at the house.

'Here?' Jazz is going. 'Here? What's here?'

'Just someone. A woman.'

'What's her name?'

'I don't know,' Tom says, as he makes his way to where the railings stop and the high wall begins.

'Where are you – What are you doing?' cries Jazz as Tom hoists himself up on to the high garden wall. 'Come down! What are you doing?'

'Come on. It's the only way in. Come on. Climb.'

'I can't climb. I'm not going to. Get down.'

'No. You've got to do it. It's the only way.'

Jazz is looking up and down the street. But this is Sunday afternoon. There's no one about, no one but Jazz to make Tom get down.

'Why can't we go in by the gate?' Jazz wants to know.

'Because this is the way in. It's the only way in. Now come on.'

'I'm too weak for this,' Jazz is going. She's trembling, hauling herself up, Tom's sitting up top of the wall dragging her up. 'I'm too weak for this.'

'Come on,' Tom's going, hoisting her. Jazz is scrabbling up the wall all legs and skinny arms like a puppet with a string missing.

Tom drags her up to where he's sitting. But no sooner is she up and she's over, slipping clean off the top down into the garden taking her brother with her.

The two of them end up tangled in a puppet-heap by

the wall. They lie there a few moments with their limbs locked, too dazed and confused to know even if they're hurt or not.

They're hurt. Of course they are. You don't come off a wall the size of that one in that way without smacking yourself pretty hard against the ground. The grass is long, really long, as it is everywhere in that overgrown orchard, but it isn't soft enough to stop that horrible sickening slap against the ground as two bodies crash down.

They lie there wondering what's hit them for a few moments.

'You stupid idiot,' Jazz finally lets out to the sky, her bony backside giving her some suddenly desperate gyp. 'Get off me you idiot.'

'Me the idiot?' Tom goes, his shoulder nearly put out of joint. 'Me the idiot? You dragged us off the top, you useless—'

'Get off me!'

'Give me a chance. Ow!'

'Ow yourself. Get off bonehead.'

'I don't know why I'm bothering with you,' Tom says, rubbing his shoulder, moving his arm, just to be sure it still does move.

'I wish you wouldn't,' Jazz goes. 'I just wish everyone could just leave me alone, that's what I wish.'

'Well no one's going to,' Tom tells her as they're wading their way through the long grasses.

'What's going to happen,' Jazz is asking, 'when we get in there anyway? What's this woman supposed to be able to do?'

'Just come on,' Tom goes, trudging through the long cobweb grass. 'Just come on.'

'Well, what's she supposed to be able to do? What is she, some kind of witch-doctor or something?'

She's some kind of witch, Tom's thinking to himself, I don't know about a doctor. She's some kind of witch, he's thinking, who's going to put a spell on you, you skinny wreck, he's thinking.

He doesn't say that though. He just tells the skinny wreck to get a move on, to follow him.

She's kicking through the grass, skinny as a blade of grass herself, nearly lost amongst the Jazz-high blades she's kicking through.

'I don't know what I'm doing here,' she's going, moaning away to herself like crazy.

You don't know what you're doing anywhere, Tom's thinking to himself. He still doesn't say anything, other than to tell the rake to get a move on, before the wind starts and blows her away.

'I'll blow you away in a minute,' she goes. But she's half-hearted. She has no enthusiasm. She has no enthusiasm for anything, it seems to Tom, other than when he really really gets on her nerves, then she finds the enthusiasm to claw his face and to slap. She still finds that kind of enthusiasm, when she wants to.

Right now though, nothing. The sun comes out and shines down on her. She squints.

Tom thinks she looks all wrong in the sunshine, the vampire that she is. Tom thinks the sun will shrivel and burn her up and the late summer September warm breeze will scatter her like ashes.

Tom thinks Jazz looks as though she thinks so too.

'There's no one here,' Jazz says, looking up at the front of the big house.

It does seem that way. All the wooden shutters are

closed over all the windows. That's not unusual, except for that small window up at the top. That one's usually open. Not now though. All closed. Shut. The big door knocker just echoes through the place as Tom smashes it against the door. It sounds as if the whole place is empty.

'There's no one here,' Jazz says again. 'I don't know why you're bothering to keep knocking.'

'Because,' says Tom, 'she always takes a long time to—'

But he stops mid-sentence. He's knocking against the door still, but as he does so, the door slowly swings open. He shoves it. It swings aside, creaking like a horror-movie coffin-lid.

'Spooky,' Jazz goes.

Tom peers into the house, looking for the spooky grey woman in her white robes. Thinking about her, he's suddenly reminded of that book they did at school about the woman with snakes for hair who could turn people to stone by looking at them. *Myth of Medusa* it was called. Tom had been really fascinated, especially by the illustration on the front, Medusa looking weird and wild, her hair a tangled mass of serpents. He still had the book somewhere in the bottom of his school-bag.

But now, with her absence, a spooky tingle, a nervousness of the dark spaces of the inside of the house out of the sun. The dark kind of hurts your eyes, just the way the light does after the cinema. You can feel the cold in there just by looking in, just by standing on the doorstep being welcomed in by no one. Spookily by no one.

'Are we going in?' Jazz asks.

Tom can feel his pulse begin to race.

'Where is she?' Tom can hear Jazz whisper from just behind him. She means the woman. 'Where is this crazy woman you want me to meet?' she's asking Tom.

He doesn't know. He only knows, as he steps into the gloom of the hall, that he has never seen this place like this. Oh, it all looks the same, only it doesn't. He's never seen it without the crazy one being there. He's never felt it quite this silent, quite this cold, quite this empty.

But Jazz is just behind him as he steps across the threshold into the dark hall. So he walks on. Jazz is just behind him, so he figures, and if she isn't bottling out, then neither is he.

Neither is he. He goes on. He's the one that's been here before. He's been here often lately. He was here last night. He was here, watching the snake. He knows his way about the place.

Over here's the pile of newspapers, over here, the same junk furniture with the stuffing out. Over everywhere, the same dust and scatter, the same disorder that always seemed, before now, so good.

'What have you brought me to?' Jazz says, looking with extreme disgust at the dust, the scatter, the good disorder. 'What kind of a person lives like this?'

They are standing just inside the big room in which Tom has spent so much time. He goes to speak, to answer his sister.

He opens his mouth.

A door slams, bang! behind them.

Bang!

They turn round with a start.

Tom can hear Jazz take a short, sharp intake of breath. He feels all the little hairs on the back of his neck stand up.

The door has slammed behind them. No one's there. Still, no one's there.

Tom and Jazz stand staring at the door. No one's there, but it feels as if there is someone. It feels as if someone's watching, watching.

Tom goes to try the door. He cannot move the handle. It will not, will not budge. 'Seems to be stuck,' he says.

'Where?' goes Jazz, coming over. 'Come out the way. Let me have a go.' She has a go. The handle won't budge. 'It's stuck,' she says.

Tom knocks on the door. 'She must be here somewhere,' he says. 'Come on, knock on the door. She's bound to hear us.'

'Why d'you bring me here?' Jazz wants to know. She's kind of hugging herself, her thin arms wrapping round her scrawny, stringy body. 'What's here? It's cold. It's damp and horrible. I hate it.'

Tom thumps against the door.

'I hate it,' Jazz goes again. 'She must be a nutter,' she says, 'to live like this.'

'And you're not a nutter to live like you do I suppose,' Tom says to her.

'That's different.'

'Is it?'

'What's in that cage?' Jazz asks, only just now noticing the thing hanging there.

'That's the snake,' Tom tells her.

Jazz shudders. 'Keep it away from me. Why *have* you brought me here?'

Tom wanders over to the cage. It is empty. He remembers the last life of the rat last night, its one loose leg twitching, the snake's black, unaffected eye.

But the snake is not there. All there is of it, is a sloughed skin, a shed skin like a transparent cobweb version of the terrible wild beast now but a husk, dried and dead for ages since.

Jazz, while Tom is looking with wonder at the snake's lost skin, has wandered over to the desk. She picks up the newspaper lying there. She begins to read. Her brow furrows.

Jazz screams.

She drops the newspaper as if it's suddenly on fire. She staggers back, her eyes darting, a succession of smaller shrieks skittering from her throat.

Tom runs up to his sister. 'What's the matter? What's the matter?'

'Get us – Just get us out of here!'

Jazz runs like a wild fire to the door, shakes at it. 'Get us out!' she screams.

Tom shouts, 'What's the matter? What's the matter?'

'The newspaper!' Jazz shrieks. 'Look at the newspaper! The newspaper!'

Jazz is losing it. She's huddled, whiter than white, her big starved eyes bulging. The look of her sends shivers all down Tom's back. The sound of her scares him.

'The newspaper!'

Tom goes over to the table. The house is darker than Tom ever remembers seeing it. The mad woman's absence madder than her being there. Tom creeps over to the desk while Jazz folds down, almost near hysterics, trembling, pointing at the newspaper lying there, just there, where she's pointing.

Tom looks where she's pointing.

He looks at the newspaper.

He gawps at the newspaper.

He gags.

He feels sick.

The newspaper. On its front, the big letters, the massive headlines that read:

TWO DIE IN MYSTERY STARVATION PACT

Under the big-lettered headlines, a picture of the crazy lady's big old house.

Under the photo, the report.

It begins: A bizarre death-pact was discovered as a sister and brother are found starved to death locked in this old disused house in . . .

Jazz screams. She can't get the door open.

Tom screams. He runs at the door.

They are a sister and brother. They are locked in this old disused house. They cannot get out.

They are going to die. Of starvation.

They are going to die.

PART FOUR

Monday and What Happened Last Night

Monday

Monday morning. What? Mad?

Its the usual. Another mad Monday. No one can get up. No one in the world can get up Monday mornings. The weekend's only just got you used to not getting up, what happens? Monday morning. No one can get up.

Especially in Tom's house. Especially today.

Suddenly, someone realises just how late it is. Then it's bedlam. Then it's really Monday morning.

Tom's trying to have a bit of a wash, but with the old man and Jazz on at him from the other side of the door to hurry up.

'Are you reading in there?' the old man's shouting through the wood. 'Tom? Are you reading in there?'

'No,' goes Tom, picking up an old United programme from the shelf where he'd left it.

Then Jazz is smashing at the door. 'Hurry up you loser! What's the matter with you?'

What's the matter with you? Tom's thinking to himself, flicking through the pages of the match programme.

But Tom knows what the matter is with his sister. She's up the wall.

Tom stuffs the folded programme into his back pocket. He opens the door. Jazz is there, waiting in the doorway.

They come face to face.

For a moment Tom expects to be attacked in some way. She's done it so many times in the past. He flinches slightly. But Jazz, looking him straight in the eye, smiles. She smiles as if he's all right. As if *she's* all right.

'Hurry up you lot,' their mum's calling from downstairs. 'You're going to be late for school.'

Tom glances away from his sister. But as he does, she takes a hold of him, kind of dances with him.

As she does, the old man appears at the bathroom door. He appears over Jazz's shoulder. Tom watches him as he watches them. He watches as Jazz lets her brother go, as Tom leaves the bathroom, as she closes the door.

The old man watches Tom disappearing down the stairs. He shakes his head.

Kids, he's thinking. Kids. Mad, or what?

What?

Then, downstairs, Tom doesn't really have time for any breakfast. Still, that's never stopped him. He compromises on the mixture this morning, pushed as he is for time. No time to let the milk get really brown.

'You'll have to hurry up,' his mum's telling him.

Tom hears the front door go. That's Jazz away. No breakfast as usual.

'No breakfast as usual,' Tom's mum's telling him, about his sister. You're telling me, he's thinking. He shovels his cereal home.

'I wish we could get her to eat like you,' she tells him. 'I'm beginning to get worried about Jazz. She's too thin.'

'Who's too thin?' the old man wants to know as he comes bustling in. 'Where're the keys? – I'm going to be late for work.'

'Jazz,' Tom's mum says.

'What about her? Have you seen those blasted keys? Who had them last?'

'You did.'

'Where the – I'm going to be so late. And so are you,' he says, to Tom, who's on the milk-dregs, slupping them off his spoon.

'She's far too thin,' Tom's mum says. 'Have you looked in your pocket?'

'Why should I look in my pocket? What, you think I was wearing this suit all over the weekend do you? In my pocket? Who's too thin?'

'Jazz.'

'You can't be too thin at that age, can you Tom?'

Tom shrugs.

The old man goes off to work, having located the keys in his pocket where he'd already picked them up and placed them. He can't see further than his nose, further than his pocket, further than his morning paper or the bottom of his tea cup. He's out of it.

Tom watches his mother. She thinks her daughter is too thin, that's all. Just too thin.

Tom gets out of there. Parents, eh? What are they like? I mean, just what are they *like*?

Tom gets himself out of there and down the road. No sign of Jazz, but plenty of the twins. The Bainsies are there like a double shot, waiting for Tom.

He's down the road, Tom, his school-bag falling to pieces, his Monday morning hair sticking up at the back. The Bainsies are there like twin parrots suddenly on both his shoulders. They want as if to peck at his ears. They've got something with which to peck at him.

'You wait till Whitbread gets hold of you.'

'You're gonna bottle it.'

'You're for it Ratty.'

'He's after your blood.'

—— 95 ——

One after the other after the other do they peck and poke threats into his ears. They're having a great time. Tom isn't. He hurries on, his head going down.

But the Bainsies are up for it. They can't let this go that easily.

'Whitbread's after you like anything.'

'You should have seen him Friday, after you ran away.'

'You should have seen him.'

'He was mad.'

'He was mad after your blood.'

'You're a goner.'

'When Whit gets his hands on you.'

So Tom downs his head still further. He legs it. The Bainsies doubled-up laughter cackles at his back as Tom goes for the school gates. Up ahead he can see Jazz.

At least she's at school today. At least she's not after sloping away home for the sickbag pig out at the chocolate drawer and the monster hawk afterwards. At least she's not after that this morning. Maybe she's going to get better? Maybe she's sick of doing what she told Tom last night she'd been doing.

What Happened Last Night

But last night, you've never seen anything like it.

There was a newspaper on the desk with that report on its front page. The front page report about a brother and sister being killed – no, dying, of starvation. Dying of starvation, there, trapped in that old decaying house where the mad woman wasn't. She wasn't there, the mad woman. The house was empty. No nutter, no snake. Just its sloughed skin.

They'd screamed. You've never heard anything like it. They'd screamed and run round the room rattling at the doors, thumping at the windows trying to get out. They couldn't get out.

The place was dark. It was growing darker by the second. Darker, colder, more horrible. It was icy, damp, stinking like the grave, like a tomb.

Jazz screamed, 'Get me out! Get me out!'

Tom screamed, 'Aagh!'

Tom kicked at the door that was jammed shut on them. He booted it better than a United striker. But that door wasn't giving in so easily. That room, that house, it was built an age ago. It was built in the time when things were built big and heavy. That was a big heavy door Tom was kicking against. It wasn't going anywhere.

'Get me out!' Jazz was screaming.

Tom was screaming, 'Help! Help!'

Jazz was screaming, 'Help! We're going to die! We're going to die!'

They really thought they were going to die.

The report was in the newspaper there on the desk.

There was Jazz, going into one. 'Get us out! Get us out!'

There was Tom, into one of his own. He was smashing away at the door. No go.

He was smashing away at the walls, at the cabinets.

Jazz ran up to the desk with the newspaper on it. She upended it. She picked it up from one end, sent it spinning over on to its back. The papers went flying.

Papers were flying all over the place where Tom was away round the room dumping stuff everywhere. He was pushing piles of books over, smashing table lamps, chucking the piled-up newspapers everywhere.

The paper from the table Jazz had upended was lost immediately amongst the carnage. Jazz gave out this fearsome scream as she kicked over the snake's cage. The sloughed snake's skin floated through the air.

Tom picked up a chair.

'Smash the window!' Jazz screamed at him.

Tom threw the chair at the window. The window smashed. But all the huge wooden shutters were up. The glass went, but the chair bounced back in off the heavy shutter.

Jazz picked up a metal lampstand. She smashed it into the shutters.

Tom could see she was out of her mind with fear. Tom was as well, but he could see Jazz was wild with it, as crazy and wild as the woman and her snake combined.

Jazz looked like an animal fighting for its life.

Shivers were running up and down Tom's back. They accelerated as Jazz screamed yet again.

Tom picked up the heavy metal lampstand. He strode over to the broken shuttered window. He braced himself.

Monday

So Tom's skulking way over the other side come breaktime, right over with the first-years and the gimps who couldn't play footie or couldn't run or fight or anything. Tom's skulking round the outside of the playground watching the soft boys, the floppies, the talcum-powdered mathematicians under their bad mum-and-dad haircuts. Tom usually laughs at this lot. Usually he takes the mick out of them. Not today. He feels like one of them. He *looks* like one of them, the way he skulks and cringes at every glimpse of the Bainsies over there pointing him out to everybody.

Tom's keeping his profile low, very low, for this week at least. He hasn't seen hide nor hair nor hammer of Whitbread, of big Dim-Whit yet today. He's hoping Dim's not at school. Which, as it happens, is nothing unusual. You're more likely to find Whit not there, if you *can* find someone who's not there. Which you can't.

But Tom wants to find the big dumb blob not there today. He wants to find him not there tomorrow, the rest of the week. Tom wants always to find Whit not there. He wants that more than anything at this moment.

That's why he skulks and scrapes over at the perimeter out of the way, just in case he finds Whit not not there. Because if Whit is not not there, the big dumb ox is going to find Tom all right. Tom knows it. He skulks. He scrapes. He watches the mumsy boys in their razor-creased school trousers and their Y-fronts and shiny shoes. He feels for them. And for himself.

Plenty of people have noticed what he's doing. They notice because the Bainsies are more than a little bit busy making people notice.

Tom doesn't know if Whit's there or not. He hasn't seen him, so he supposes not. Still, you can't be too careful, can you?

Then the bell goes for the end of the break. The

football game finishes. Kids start to disappear. The playground empties.

Tom's new mates, the shiny-shoed boys with brief-cases like pretend lawyers file out first, leaving him on his own. He was on his own anyway, but now he's looking like he's on his own. He's looking like a loner is Tom, shuffling along behind everybody. He doesn't have a mate in the world, let alone in this school – no one friendly or foolish enough to stand with him against Big Dim Whit. Not even Egg, who's keeping a well low profile himself.

Tom waits until just about everyone's gone before he follows on. Whitbread doesn't seem to be there any-where.

Tom dodges round the corner once he's peeked round it, just in case. But all's still safe.

Safe? What? Does this feel safe, or what?

How long can he keep this up?

And if he manages to avoid Whit today, what about tomorrow? What about the next day? What about after school, in the street, round the corner well out of the way of any teacher or anyone likely to break it up before Tom gets his face broken?

Safe? Where's safe, when things are like this?

Safe? How can you ever feel safe when every other second you feel sick because you don't know who's on your side or who's against you?

Safe? It isn't fair.

Nowhere's safe.

What Happened Last Night

Last night Jazz had told Tom what she'd been doing.

They were over the park together. They were sitting on the old roundabout they'd known and played on for ever. They were sitting side by side on the thing, keeping it creeping round with the odd touch on the ground with their feet.

As they span slowly, ever so slowly round, Jazz told Tom what she'd been doing. She tried to tell him why as well. She tried to put it into words why she'd stopped eating for such a long time, why she felt the need to pig out so disgustingly on chocolate, and then chuck up.

They'd run into the park together, having smashed the whole of the heavy wooden shutter off the window of the old house. They'd smashed their way out. The shutter had splintered open, swung falling away to let in the blessed low light of the September late afternoon.

The sun had shone through the fruit trees of the overgrown garden as Tom and Jazz had leapt from the smashed open window. Down they'd leapt, thudding together into the long grass at the end of the summer.

This was it. They were away, the two of them, off across the wild wide grass, up the wall as if it wasn't six foot but two, and down the other side. They ran away without question, without another look back or second thought. They ran side by side silently through the silent September Sunday afternoon streets until they made the park.

The park was like a sanctuary. It was a safe place, a place they'd always known for ever.

There they were able to stop. Their breaths were

there, they were able to catch them. But it took a long time. It was a time spent doubled over holding the belly, blowing out all the panic and the fear, grabbing back the air.

Eventually the air took back over. They calmed down. Eventually they made their way over to the old roundabout. Without talking about it they sat down on it, starting it slowly off with the odd touch of their feet on the ground.

The beautiful sun was low by now, really low. But there was still a great warmth.

Without talking about it, they waited for the warmth to encourage them.

Without Tom mentioning it, Jazz started to tell him about it. She started to tell him what it was like.

'It's like this,' Jazz said.

They were sitting on the roundabout last night, turning slowly in the warm sun. It felt like the last sun of summer, the last day before the cold and damp and dark.

But now it wasn't dark. It was still light. It had been dark, in that crazy woman's ghost house. But now it was light again, still just about summer. They were on the roundabout in the park they'd known ever since they could know anything.

They felt warm.

'It's like this,' Jazz told Tom, last night, on the roundabout, turning slowly, unwinding, slowly letting it all out.

Tom had to wait a while while Jazz gathered together what it was all about. 'It's like this,' she said. Then she said nothing. Tom waited. He waited a long while. But he would have waited a much longer while if need be.

He could see how difficult, how painful it was for his sister to put her illness into words for him. But he could also tell how important it was for her to do so. So he waited.

The roundabout stopped still.

'It's like,' Jazz said, 'it's like – when – you know, when there's nothing you can do about everyone not liking you.'

Last night, sat still on the still roundabout, Jazz told Tom what it was like to not feel safe – to feel no one liked you because you were – just because you were what you were.

Tom wanted to tell Jazz she was wrong. Tom knew that people liked Jazz. But she didn't know, because she'd stopped liking herself.

'You wonder why. You wonder what's wrong with you,' she told him. 'You wonder what's wrong with you when you don't seem to have a good time any more. And you look at yourself and see how fat and stupid you are and if anyone's having a good time anywhere they're the thin people and the good looking people – because that's how it looks Tom. That's how it looks.'

Tom shook his head. He was thinking of all the ugly footballers he could name, lots of them, who seemed to be having a good time, from what Tom could see. But he didn't say anything. It didn't seem the right time somehow, to start talking football and footballers, even those that aren't so handsome, but were brilliant on the ball and so were much, much more cool than any boy-bands and spicy-girls who weren't much good for anything other than posing and pouting. But Tom didn't say anything. This was Jazz's turn, her time to speak. Tom didn't want to break the spell.

'Then you have a good look at yourself,' Jazz went on, 'a good look. There's nothing to find. You see what you see. You have to change it. You have to change it. You have to do something to it. Hurt it. Damage it. So you pig. Then you feel disgusting. It's disgusting. So you get sick. It feels like you're damaging the right thing. It feels right to make it sick.

'But the damage doesn't last. You feel better, which makes you feel worse. Because all you can do is hate yourself.

'Do you know what I mean Tom?' she asked him, looking at him through the low sunlight. 'Do you know what I mean?'

Tom looked down at the ground. He didn't want to have to answer. There was nothing he could say. He didn't really understand. He wanted to, but didn't get it. Slobs like Dim Whitbread ought to be the ones hating themselves, not ordinary, proper people like Jazz and himself.

'Nowhere,' Jazz went on, 'nowhere's safe from yourself, when it's like that. I mean, when you hate yourself that much – when all you can do to get back is to – not to get back – to get better is to try to change, alter, do so much . . .

'You try to do so much to yourself Tom, do you understand? You try to do so much to yourself because you think – you feel you're ugly and everyone hates you – you try to do so much to yourself, it's nearly like – as if you wanted to do away with yourself. That's how it feels.

'That's how it feels to cram and cram with chocolate, because you've failed to change. That's how it feels Tom. It's stupid, I know, but that's how it feels.'

Monday

Nowhere's safe.

And it isn't. Especially when you've begun to reckon you might've just got away with it for today, just when your mind starts to wander back to yesterday about what your sister told you about hating herself for something, and that feeling of nowhere being safe from the feeling, when you-know-who appears round the corner under the cover of the links.

You do know who, don't you?

You know, don't you, that Tom's been skulking out of the way of the big bronto-brain Whitbread. Him.

Suddenly, with Tom's mind just wandering for half a second back to last night, from under the links, the overhead corridors, from under there appears big Dim-Whit followed by a couple of sneering Bainsies, followed by a heap of followers, followed by about half the rest of the school. But no adults to be seen. No teachers – where were they ever, when you needed them?

It was as if they'd all legged it from Big Dim. As would Tom, given half the chance. But half- even a quarter-chance, he would not be given. Not this time. Before he could realise it, Whit was on him, towering over him, with the Bainsies and their followers blocking every possible exit.

'Hello Ratty,' said Big witty Dim.

You'd have to think he was a bit of a comedian and all, the way they all laugh like they're about to die from Whit's superior wit.

Tom glances about. Nothing but grinning, spiteful faces does he see here. Nothing but enemies does he see

– some of them he'd considered friends, until now, until Whitbread turned their heads.

Strangely, Tom seems to have time to wonder. He wonders what he'd be doing now, if this was one of his mates being threatened by something so threatening and convincing as Whit.

'I've been looking for you,' Whit says.

'Have you?' Tom goes.

'Yeah. Cause I owe you something.'

'That's all right,' Tom says to him, 'you have it. Give it to your best mate as a Christmas present.'

Tom listens to the laughter, the nervousness of it. He sees, out of the corner of his eyes, the excited squirming of some of the boys he had thought of as his mates. He even sees Egg there.

He doesn't hate them for what they're doing. They all look like him. They all look like Toms, squirming with fear and excitement because someone, not themselves, is going to get it.

They aren't to blame.

Nowhere's safe.

'That's what I hate about you Ratty,' big Dim-Whit's telling Tom. 'You're such a smarmy little rat – you know that?'

But Tom's not bothering to answer. Leastways, he's trying to make it look as if he's not bothering. The truth is, he *can't* answer. His mouth's gone as dry as an electric blanket. His throat's as if it's swollen. His jaw's locked as tight as if it really is locked and he has thrown away the key. But he stands there trying to look not bothered.

'What's the matter with you Ratty?' Whit wants to know. 'Cat got your tongue?'

'Rat's got his tongue,' a voice comes from one side.

Tom thinks it sounds like a Bains. He wouldn't be at all surprised. Typical.

'What do I have to do, punch it out of you?' Whit asks, advancing.

Tom tries to step back. He realises he's been stepping back for some while, while Whit's been stepping up, looming over him. Tom's back now right up against it. There are Bainsies to his left and right – Bainsies and Dim-Whits everywhere, locking him in. He backs harder against the wall, friendless. On his own.

Big grinning Dim looms over him. Tom gets ready to do down. Whit's grinning looks real nasty, really spiteful. This is going to be bad. This is going to be really bad.

'This is going to be really good,' Dim-Whit goes, removing his jacket. 'I've been really looking forward to this,' he's going, making a real nasty exhibition of rolling up his shirt sleeves.

'I'm gonna punch your lights out,' he says. 'Who's to stop me?'

What Happened Last Night

'It's as if you want to do away with yourself,' Jazz told Tom on the roundabout, when they were safe.

Tom was silent. For a long while, they were both silent. The sun was going down, silently.

'But why didn't you want to just talk about it?' Tom said at last.

'Who's to talk to?' Jazz asked. 'There isn't anybody.'

'There is now,' said Tom.

Jazz looked at him, long, hard.

'There's me,' he said to his sister.

Monday

'I'm gonna punch your lights out,' Whit says. 'Who's to stop me?'

'There's me,' this other voice goes, from the other side.

Tom doesn't get it for a moment. He hears the voice, the girl's voice, but he doesn't get it.

'You touch him,' the voice goes, 'you're going to have to deal with me too.'

Tom watches Whit's face turn in the direction of the voice.

Tom realises it is Jazz's voice. He turns. She has stepped forward to the front of the crowd.

Whit laughs. 'And what you reckon you going to be able to do about it, you worm?'

'I'm going to be able to do plenty.'

'Yeah? Like what?'

'Like wreck your ugly face,' Jazz goes.

'Jazz,' Tom says.

'You wanna watch it and all,' Big ugly Whit says to Jazz, the grin slipping off his face.

'And so do you,' another voice goes from behind Whit's back. Whit turns round.

Lin Adams, one of Jazz's mates, has also stepped to the front.

'What you say?' says Whit.

'I say,' says Lin, 'that you wanna watch it. Cause I got it in for you as well.'

'Oh have you now?'

Then, from the back, people are shoved well and truly out of the way. From the back appears the fourteen hairy great stone of Isabell Harris, Jazz's not-mate, Jazz's great enemy. Jazz hates Isabell, and has always thought that Isabell hated her.

But Isabell thuds up to the front of the crowd, fixes Whit in the eye and says, 'And so have I.'

And Whit doesn't smile. No way.

'And so has she,' Isabell goes to this other girl, 'haven't you Chris? You got it in for this ugly tub and all, haven't you?'

'Yeah,' goes Chris.

'And me,' this other girl goes. Then another. Then another. Then another after another.

Whit's just about surrounded now, his mates, the Bainsies especially, having evaporated like little wisps of steam.

Whit lets out a little semi-smile. 'Got all your girl-friends to protect you Ratty, eh?'

Fourteen stones of Isabell Harris shudders forward. 'I ain't no one's girl-friend,' she says. 'But I'll tell you what,' she says, 'you lay a finger on Tom, or Jazz, or any of my mates, we'll get you, you piece of – get out of here,' she goes, swinging a Doc Marten at Whit's disappearing backside.

Wit has to leg it through the crowd, about half the girls there taking a boot at his trembling buttocks.

Everyone's laughing.

Whit runs clean out of school.

Isabell goes to walk away.

'Hey, Isabell,' Jazz goes to her, 'thanks.'

Isabell just nods. The group is dispersing. As they go, the girls give Jazz's shoulder a squeeze, or ruffle her hair, or just smile at her.

In the end, all that's left is Tom, still up against the wall, and Jazz. That's all there is.

'Are you going to get better now?' Tom asks her.

'I don't know,' she says. 'I can't tell.'

Tom goes into his pocket. He fishes out a muesli bar. He holds it out to his sister.

Jazz glances to one side. She looks irritated. 'It isn't as simple as that,' she says.

'I don't care,' he tells her.

She shakes her head. 'Don't you? I do. Come on, we'll be late for lessons.'

'I don't care,' Tom tells her.

'No,' she says, 'but I do. I've got a lot of catching up to do.'

Jazz turns and walks into the school building.

Tom stands looking all round him. There's no one left. Except himself. He's standing there now on his own so suddenly, almost left wondering what happened. Tom's left wondering how it is that things change so suddenly, so absolutely.

Tom's left wondering why he seems to have no power over anything. How it all seems to happen around him, and to him. But never because of him.

There are, it seems to Tom, two types of person in this world. Those that make things happen, and those that have things happen to them.

He wonders why. And how can you change it?

He looks around. There's no one left but him.

He thinks about the crazy woman, her wild grey hair.

As he thinks of her, he remembers the story of Medusa, with wild snakes growing from her head. She could change people to stone by looking at them.

That's how it feels to Tom. He feels as if he has turned to stone, with no power to do anything about anything. That's exactly how Tom feels. Like a statue of stone, just about to crumble.

PART FIVE

Friday and What Happened Last Night

Friday

Friday morning again.

Mad?

But mad in a very different kind of way.

Tom's awake. Early.

The weather's gone. It's September properly now, overcast, with an autumn wind. The apples are falling, bruising on to the ground. Everything's winding down. Tom feels it.

He lies awake before anybody else has moved. The whole house is silent. Still. Spooky. It's as if everyone else has gone somewhere. Everyone except Tom, who might as well be alone here, as everywhere else.

What Happened Last Night

Plenty. I can tell you.

All of it crazy. Really mad.

But before that, every other night this week. What happened Monday night, Tuesday, Wednesday?

Nothing. Like a suspended animation. Nothing happening day after day, night after night. Thursday night, last night, found Tom lingering outside the crazy woman's house, watching through the railings as a new shutter was fitted on the big window downstairs.

Tom had stood there like this on every other night,

but had seen nothing. The broken shutter hung by one hinge, the glass behind boarded over.

Now on Thursday night the glass is back in, a new shutter going up. Tom watched the work in progress, aching to climb the wall, to run the length of the orchard, now with its long grasses madly hacked back, to the house. To find the wild woman, her snake-hair like Medusa, ready to turn onlookers to stone.

Tom thought about that old story, Medusa, with snakes for hair, with the ability to turn people to stone. Tom feels the cold heart of stone deep inside himself, with everything so altered around him, everything so spoilt. Because now, after Monday, nothing is the same.

Shivers ran down Tom's spine. The weather had turned to autumn, the sky showed it, the wind told of it, but Tom shivered at the idea of Medusa's snake-hair stoning every good to very bad.

Because that was what had happened. Tom's life had been turned upside-down.

At school, every day, Jazz, the crazy girl, the Bulimia-Nervosian, every day surrounded by friends, by girls she never knew were her friends, by girls she had always thought of as enemies. Jazz didn't seem to have any enemies now. She was the centre of attention. And why?

Not only because of what had happened with Dim-Whit. That was part of it, but only a small part. The main thing was – Jazz suffered from bulimia nervosa!

Now Jazz was supposed to be wanting to get better, everyone got to know about it. And did they ever want to get to know about it!

Jazz became like a walking soap opera, a star in her own right, the most popular and famous person in the whole school. It was as if all the others, all the girls anyway, it was as if they were in a way jealous, as if being sick after pigging out on two tons of chocolate was the most romantic thing a person of Jazz's age and sex could do.

Weird, or what?

Tom couldn't make it out.

Even big brutish Isabell wanted some of it. Even she thought Jazz was it. You know, really *it*.

Tom thought some of them were so keen, so envious, they looked like they wanted to go off and get bulimia nervosa themselves, if only they knew how. Tom thought they looked as if they were hanging, clinging on to Jazz's every word trying to find out how to go about getting the glamorous and desirable disease.

They wouldn't be so keen, Tom thought, watching Jazz flushed with pride and popularity, if they had seen her in the states he had. They wouldn't be so keen, Tom knew, if they could get a whiff of the chocolate-sick and congealed milk resulting from all that glamour.

But Jazz's emaciated – half-starved – look looked suddenly stylish, very cool. Jazz herself was swanning around still not really eating anything, behaving like the Soap star she'd become.

While Tom – what of him?

He watched. Only that. Nothing else.

Tom watched his sister swanning in and out of the school refectory displaying her desperately glamorous secret. He watched her friends and her old enemies admiring her, wanting to be like her.

Tom watched his own mates, his own old enemies. He watched them playing football, watched them messing about, watched them laughing and talking and eating and running. All this Tom watched from the outside. He watched from outside, excluded, left out.

Tom could feel the weight of the atmosphere gathered round him. In contrast to the interest and enthusiasm following Jazz everywhere she went, a dead halt is all that Tom could manage. Wherever *he* went, the lads all stopped, silenced, turned away.

If he tried to get involved, if he tried to join in a game of footie, especially when once he nearly scored, what would happen? Nothing. Nothing happened wherever Tom went, whatever he did.

Tom looked about at everyone crowding round his sister, then at everyone avoiding him, and there was no avoiding it. Ever since Monday, ever since Jazz and her mates had seen off Whitbread, Tom had become the outsider, the boy that couldn't fight his own battles, the loser. The grass.

Tom deserved to be where he found himself. He deserved to be left outside.

Friday

Usually mad, but, you know, OK. Friday. Usually OK, being the last day before the weekend, Friday morning going before the afternoon, the afternoon that leads up to the night, Friday, the night before Saturday glorious morning, the best day of the week.

But what's happening?

It's too early for a start. Tom can't sleep. He hasn't slept properly all week.

He isn't hungry. Tom is not hungry.

Tom Rattigan without an appetite? Mad?

Crazy, I tell you.

It doesn't add up, does it. Nothing makes sense—

But yes it does. The only thing is, Tom doesn't care for the sense it's all making, for all the bad feeling that that common sense makes.

He gets out of bed. No point in lying there any longer not sleeping, tired, but not sleepy, not feeling hungry, but feeling empty. Empty.

He gets up quietly, goes downstairs, quietly. In the kitchen, nothing. Jazz is still in bed, asleep. At least she can sleep. She's all right. And she is all right. Since Monday, she's been doing pretty good. Not eating or anything like that, but at least she's been with people. And people have been with her.

Monday, with big Dim-Whit driven out of school with Isabell's size ten DM up his backside that, you'd have thought, would have been an ending, a happy ending to all the bad things that had led up to it. You'd have thought that, wouldn't you?

So would Tom. He'd have thought he would have been safe now, without Whit wanting his face pushed through, without Jazz on a downer after him all the time. Tom would have thought that that was the end, a happy conclusion.

But, as he looks around the kitchen, as he remembers Jazz face down in her own sick-spittle on the table, when she needed his help and not he hers, as Tom thinks about his big mixture of a breakfast he feels quite sick at the prospect, Tom thinks – Tom thinks this isn't the end to anything. This is the beginning. And there's worse to come.

Much worse.

What Happened Last Night

Monday, Tuesday, Wednesday, Thursday night, last night. Every night Tom walked home on his own, feeling like a worm, feeling like a wimp. Ashamed, like a grass. Nobody, but nobody wanted anything to do with him. Even Egg – even his probably best mate – even he let Tom go by on his own. Egg was just like the rest of them. Since the other day, since Monday, not one of them could bear to look properly at him.

Every night this week Tom had left the school straight after school, made his way straight home. No football, nothing. Straight home, where Jazz would make a pretty good job of avoiding him now she was it, and where the dumb parents were just as dumb and self-involved and as ignorant and mad as ever.

Everyone's mad.

Ever since Tom realised just how mad everyone was, he'd felt like an outsider. He'd felt scared, Tom – what was so mad about feeling scared? Nothing. It's the sanest, most horrible state to be in. And nearly impossible to get out of.

Thursday night came. Tom sloped scared out of school on his own again. He didn't say anything to anybody. He simply left to get away from the oppression of no one saying anything to him or looking properly at him.

Thursday night and Tom made his way home on his own. The weather was not good. The summer had gone, for good. The darkness was on its way.

Tonight, Thursday night, Tom stood outside the railings of the big old house on the corner. He was peering through the brown leaves of the fruit trees to the house where a new window-shutter was being fitted, when his sister's voice appeared beside him almost before she did.

'She set us up,' she said to Tom, 'didn't she?'

Tom looked round at her, quite startled. She'd come out of nowhere, like the crazy woman did, like Medusa did with her hair and house full of snakes.

Jazz nodded towards the old house where two workmen were finishing off the new shutter.

'Will you go back?' she said.

Tom looked over. 'I can't, can I? Think of all the damage we did.'

Jazz smiled. 'Yeah. We nearly wrecked the place, didn't we?'

Tom said, 'Nearly? We smashed just about everything in sight.'

'She set us up though,' Jazz said.

'Did she? Do you think so?'

'Don't you?'

They both looked over at the house. Tom wanted to ask Jazz if she'd ever heard of the story of the woman with snakes for hair who could damage people, change them simply by looking at them.

'Her name's Jones,' Jazz suddenly said.

Tom looked back at her. 'Jones.'

'Liz Argent in my year, her dad knows someone who knows her. Mrs Jones she's called.'

'Mrs?'

'Yeah. Her husband died. I've been asking around. She used to be somebody.'

'What do you mean?'

'She used to be something, I don't know what. She

used to be important. Something happened to her. She cracked up.'

'She cracked up?'

'Went mad. Nervous breakdown. Cracked up.'

Tom looked across to the house, to the repaired shutter, the concentration apparent on his face.

'She began to think she was someone else,' Jazz went on. 'Turned into a right schizo apparently.'

'Who did she think she was?' Tom said, seriously.

'Who? I don't know.'

'I do,' Tom said, dead serious. 'I know who. Look at this,' he said, fishing about in his bag. He withdrew the book they'd been working on in school. *Myth of Medusa*.

'Look,' he said, 'look at this.'

Jazz looked at the book. 'What of it?'

'What of it? Look who it's by. Look.'

Jazz read the name of the author on the front of the book. 'Jennifer Jones?'

'Jennifer Jones,' Tom, dead seriously, said. 'It's her. *Myth of Medusa*.'

'What?'

'That's who she is. Don't you see it? *Myth of Medusa*. Jennifer Jones. She wrote it. That's who she thinks she is – Medusa. She can turn people to stone by looking at them. Her hair's snakes. Some bloke – Perseus I think – he makes her look at herself in his shield. That's the only way. It turns it all back on herself. That's what it is Jazz. Don't you see it?'

Tom, excited, waving the book in front of his sister's nose, stopped at the sight of her face. They stood looking at each other for a few moments.

'Don't you see it?' Tom said to her.

Another moment of Jazz's incredulous face ticked by.

She shook her head. 'What are you talking about?' she said.

'Listen,' Tom went on, 'Jennifer Jones. It's her. I know it is. She wrote the book. It – she went – she cracked up – you said so! I've seen the PC on her desk. Why else would a nutter like her have a brand new PC on the desk and a snake and—'

'What are you talking about?' Jazz said, turning a circle in exasperation. 'What are you *on*?'

'It's her!' Tom shouted at her. 'I know it is!'

'You're – you are off your head,' Jazz went, stepping away from him. 'You're madder than she is. Do you know that?' she said, beginning to walk away from him.

'Oh,' he called after her, 'and you're not I suppose. You – just because you think you're it now!'

Jazz was walking away, shaking her head.

'Just because you think you're it,' Tom was shouting after her. 'Just because you reckon you're something. Well you're not!' he was shouting.

'You're not,' he found himself saying. 'You're not anything,' he was saying, to himself, surprised to find his tears falling, splashing on to the covers of *Myth of Medusa*, on to the illustration, the snake-haired woman looking out into his unshielded face.

Friday

There's much worse to come.

There has to be, because nothing's the same. Everything's changed – but for the worse. Nothing resolved.

No end to any of it. It all goes on and on, getting worse and worse.

Tom sits himself down at the table. There doesn't seem to be anything left worth looking forward to. There doesn't seem to exist the possibility of a hunger that isn't marred, spoiled by fear and people's poor opinion and parental failure. And everything going wrong. Granite effigies that were once people, changed for ever by what has gone wrong.

Tom sits at the table remembering how everything, but everything can go wrong. He remembers how he traipsed home last night a long way behind his sister. Word had got round about her illness, had got round so far and fast it had reached the ears of the teachers and the headmaster.

Tom remembers, as he sits through the too early unhungry silence of first thing Friday, being too dizzy with looking at *Myth of Medusa* to realise that Jazz was now going to have to tell their parents, before they found out from someone else.

Tom remembers only dragging on behind with the book in his hands, the Medusa myth growing ever more powerful through his clutching fingers.

He gets up from the table, goes to where the book is flung on the side, its pages open. He doesn't touch the thing, in case its magic turns and turns again, its power augmenting, changing, disrupting everything.

He looks at the book, remembering having thrown it there as the screaming reached unbearable pitch, as Jazz tugged at her own hair in frustration and fear.

'I blame you for this!' the old man had said.

He'd thundered up and down, clouting the worktops, throwing a mug into the sink. It smashed.

'That's it! That's it!' Tom's mother had shrieked at him. 'Blame me! Blame me! I knew I'd have to have the blame for this!'

'No!' Jazz had screamed.

Tom had stood there, the book in his hands.

'Well who else is to blame then?' the old man shouted, swinging round, his red face glowing.

'No!' Jazz screamed.

'How could you?' screamed her mother at her. 'How could you?'

Jazz had screamed, pulling at her own hair.

'Are you stupid?' Tom had had to shout at them, at the two of them, the dumb parents. 'Are you both mad, or what?' he'd had to shout, throwing down the book.

Myth of Medusa had bristled in all its opened pages on the side as the old man came at Tom like some sort of prize-fighter, his hands raised.

Tom had never been hit by his parents, but he thought, then, at that moment, the old man, driven to a red insanity as he was, was going to clout him round the face. Tom really thought it was going to happen. He thought he could see it – he thought he could feel it coming.

Now, in the silence of early Friday morning, the coffee mugs still shatter in the sink and on the floor, Jazz's screams still hang in the air, Tom's father's red-mad rush still stings with the coming slap and his mother's cries echo in the empty cooker.

It was mad, but violent-mad, with everyone off their heads, frantic with blaming everyone else or not wanting to be blamed – everyone crazy with the kind of horrible dislike for each other that pulls families apart.

Tom sits at the kitchen table feeling the pull of his

family disintegrating. He doesn't want it to happen. He doesn't want it to happen.

He jumps up. He goes to the side, picks up the book as if he's going to wring its neck.

He looks round.

Someone's going to answer for all this. And there's only one person *to* answer for it. Jennifer Jones. Medusa.

Tom goes out to get himself dressed. He knows now where he's going, and why.

PART SIX

Friday Night

Friday Night

She's there, in the street, but with an awful big hat containing all the usually blow-away hair. The hat is full of snakes.

He has spent the whole day – the whole day! – waiting, turning somersaults in her garden, heaped in the doorway like an old fashioned tramp out of the rain, thundering round the garden trying to keep warm. Just before lunch-time he slipped down the shops for a packet of digestives and a carton of orange. Then, straight away, back.

All day he has waited for her to appear like a vampire from her day-sleep, all day watching her windows, the shutters over the windows. But they all, all day, stayed shut. No account taken of Tom's boredom and frustration, the shutters stayed shut against him, in his face.

He'd watched the school uniforms all going down the road at home-time, but had stayed to watch the shutters shut, hard and fast in his face.

Now, making his way home, dirty and weary, here she is, in his face, her face just glancing at him for a moment with a little dry smile coming and going under her great hat.

He doesn't recognise her for an instant in that snake hat, her white, webbed gowns covered by a huge black overcoat, but she sees him coming, glances by him with a little smile. Nothing more. She doesn't speak to him, or stop, or even falter. She glances a little dry smile off him as she sees his surprised face with its shocked mouth dropping open.

Tom's mouth drops open.

She glides by him on hidden feet as silent and smooth as on wheels.

Tom reels around, too stunned to speak, to call out all the questions he has been waiting all morning and afternoon to ask her. His mouth drops open, but something unexpected seems to drop out.

'Tom,' his voice seems to say.

Only it isn't his voice. His father's voice seems for the time it takes to say Tom, to be coming from Tom's mouth.

'Tom,' the voice goes again.

But now Tom can tell that the voice is coming from beside him, from his own front garden. Tom looks round. He's there, the old man, not so red as last night, but as mad as ever in his black slip-ons and track-suit bottoms and white shirt with a tie.

'Tom,' his father's going to him, taking no notice of Medusa as she glides away under her coat.

'Jennifer!' Tom calls after her. But to no response. She slips further away. 'Mrs Jones!' he calls.

Now she halts.

Tom holds his breath.

'Tom? Who're you calling?' his dad's voice is going, just as if he cannot see the tall dark hat and coated figure in the street before them. 'Tom?'

Medusa half turns. She is going to look, to stare stone-statues into Tom's face. He feels the urge to look about for a shield, an old car wheel-hub, anything to reflect the stare, to turn it back on itself.

But Medusa doesn't fully turn to face him. She is

looking to one side, opening a little hand make-up case. She has flipped it open.

'Tom!' Tom's father's more urgent voice is calling. 'What's the matter with you? John's waiting here for you. Tom!'

But Tom's watching, watching as the weird woman flips open the make-up case, very briefly checks her hair in the mirror on the case-lid, touches it here, and here, then flips the lid closed.

Now she turns her head to fully face Tom. For an instant they are face to face. A look of understanding is flickering between them, a brief but friendly exchange of unstonelike stares.

Medusa's smile flickers before she turns away.

'Tom!' his father shouts down his ear. 'Hey!'

'What?' Tom says, snapping out of his reverie as the weird woman wheels smoothly away in her black coat and hat.

'Wake up son,' his father says. 'John's here, waiting for you.'

'John?'

'Your mate. John.'

'Oh. Egg.'

'Yes, Egg. He's indoors.'

'Is he?'

'Yes.'

They pause. Tom's in two minds whether to run after Medusa or not. He fingers the book in his pocket.

'Well?' the old man goes. 'Aren't you going in to see him?'

Tom's looking down the road to where she's just about to disappear round the corner. As he watches her, she seems to disappear *before* she gets to the corner.

—— 131 ——

'Tom?'

No answer.

'Tom?'

No answer.

'Hey! You! Snap out of it!'

Tom snaps.

'Aren't you going in to see Egg? He's been waiting for you for ages. He's got something for you. Where have you been?'

Where has he been? Tom hardly knows. He's in a daze, wandering past his father into the house, where his mother's waiting in the kitchen.

'Where have you been? It doesn't matter, Egg's in the front room waiting for you.'

'Yes, I know.'

'Well get in there and see him then.'

Tom wanders out of the kitchen in a daze. He goes into the front room. There's Egg. Tom sits down on a chair a fair bit away from him. Egg's not been near Tom all week. Tom's not going near him now.

They sit there for a few moments.

'All right?' Egg asks Tom, eventually.

Tom nods, looking down. Another few long moments pass between them with nothing said.

Eventually, Egg sighs, says, 'Tom, listen. We're sorry. You know?'

Tom looks at him.

Egg looks away. 'We're – you know – all the lads – we let you down.'

'What?' Tom says.

'It shouldn't have been like that,' Egg says, looking up again. 'It shouldn't have. We shouldn't have – you know – it was only you, you and a bunch of girls against

Whitbread. He's a nutter. You know, we were scared. Tom? Tom?'

Tom's gazing at him with his mouth popped open again.

'You all right Tom?'

'What? Yeah. I'm all right.'

'Yeah, anyway. We shouldn't have let it happen. We didn't back you – we bottled out Tom. Sorry.'

Tom shakes his head. He can't find anything to say.

'We were all – this week,' Egg goes on, 'not knowing what to say to you. We thought – well the Bainsies reckoned you were going to have a go at us—'

'Don't take any notice of those Bainsies,' Tom tells his mate Egg, 'ever. Those two – you wait till I get my hands on—'

But just then Tom's mum comes flinging in, getting herself excited about something or the other. 'If you can do what you're going to do, I can do what I'm going to do. I don't care what your father says . . .'

Jazz comes following in behind, grinning.

'Oh, hello Tom,' Jazz goes.

'Hello,' Tom goes back.

'Jazz tells me you weren't at school today,' Tom's mum then says.

Tom nearly staggers back. 'All the times you've bunked off—' he starts to go, about to start having a real go at his sister.

But, 'It's all right,' his mother tells him before he can properly go into one, 'we've sorted everything out.'

'What do you mean?' Tom asks her.

'Have you got your stuff, John?' his mum asks Egg.

Egg nods, pointing to a full carrier.

—— 133 ——

'What's happening?' Tom asks.

'Don't you know?' asks his mum.

'No.'

'Jazz is going to get proper counselling and I'm going to a hypnotist.'

'No,' Tom says, nodding at Egg's carrier. 'No, I mean – what? A hypnotist?'

'To help me give up smoking. Ask your dad about you and John.'

'Ask me what?' the old man wants to know, coming through the door.

'Haven't you told him about tomorrow?' Tom's mum asks his dad.

'No,' goes the old man. Then says nothing. In fact, no one says anything. They all stand round Tom, all four of them, the old man and woman, Jazz and Egg, all with dumb grins on about this thing they all know about and Tom doesn't.

'What is it?' he asks.

'Tell him then,' Tom's mum says to the old man.

'You tell him John,' the old man goes to Egg.

Egg grins. 'Your old m – I mean your dad's got tickets for tomorrow.'

'Tomorrow?'

'For the match,' the old man chips in.

'The match?' Tom stammers.

'United – Liverpool,' Egg goes. 'Tomorrow. Only the most important fixture of the season. And we're going. You, me and your dad.'

'That's why John's staying round tonight,' Tom's mum says.

'He can't believe it,' Jazz says.

'Believe it Tom,' goes the old man, producing the three tickets, waving them in front of Tom's face.

'I don't believe it,' Tom goes, glancing round.

He's glancing round thinking about her, Mrs Jones, Medusa, her one glance at him in the street just a few minutes ago. Just a few minutes after the one glance from her and everything's changed again. The stone statues all come back to life. Tom's life clicks back awake. He has a life. If there's one thing Tom Rattigan has, now, it is a life.

He looks back round at his family and his best friend. 'Brilliant,' he says. 'Everything's brilliant.'

'But,' goes the old man, whipping away the tickets, 'if I ever, ever find out you've been bunking off school again—'

'I won't Dad,' Tom tells him, 'ever.'

'You better not,' he goes. 'Or you Jazz.'

'Don't worry,' she says.

'Now buzz off down the park or somewhere,' goes the old man, 'get out of here till dinner's ready.'

'Give it an hour,' Tom's mum tells them.

Tom smiles. 'Come on then,' he says to Egg.

'Coming Jazz?' Egg asks her.

'Course I am,' she says.

'You are?' Tom asks her as they're going out of the house. 'You, coming to play football?'

'Course I am.'

'You're going in goal then,' he tells her.

'No I'm not. No way. I'm as good on the pitch as you are, any day.'

'No you're not.'

'She is Tom,' Egg says.

'Yeah,' says Tom, 'but you don't ever tell your own sister that, do you?'

'Oh yeah? Well you'd better be nice to me,' Jazz goes, 'or I might tell Egg about you when you used to want to do ballet dancing.'

'What?' goes Egg. 'You didn't!'

'Course I didn't,' Tom says to him. 'Come here,' he says, to Jazz, starting to chase her up the road. 'You little liar.'

'I know,' Jazz calls over her shoulder at him. 'I'm always lying. It's my hobby.'

And she runs off, laughing, with Tom after her, Egg running after Tom, laughing at him.

Tom catches her, Egg catches him. They all fall over each other, ending up heaped and laughing on the pavement.

Then, in the park, Tom stops for a breather, watches his sister beating the lads at football. He watches her flushed face, the colour in her cheeks. She's as thin as air, but moves like the wind. For an instant, he's very nearly proud of her.

Then he is proud of her.

The Bainsies are skulking nearby, waiting to see what Tom' going to do to them.

He's going to ask them to play, to join in. That's all he *can* do. He doesn't have it in him to want to get back at people, no matter what they're like.

But what *are* they like, people?

I mean, what are they *like*?

Tom beckons to the Bainsies. He shakes his head.

People, eh?

Weird, or what?

Mad, entirely, the lot of them.

Also by John Brindley

The Terrible Quin

Suddenly he moves. He grabs James . . . swings him round, throwing him over the edge . . . 'No!' Maria has screamed before she can even realise what has happened, or even that she has screamed.

Maria and James's father vanishes, without explanation. They want him back. They're desperate. But their search for him turns into a living nightmare. It's oppressive, relentless and nothing can prepare them for facing the Terrible Quin.

A gripping thriller guaranteed to have you on the edge of your seat.